BELLA ARABELLA

Liza Fosburgh

Illustrated by Catherine Stock

A BANTAM SKYLARK BOOK®

TORONTO • NEW YORK • LONDON • SYDNEY • AUCKLAND

RL 4, 007–011

BELLA ARABELLA

A Bantam Book / published by arrangement with
Four Winds/Macmillan Publishing Company

PRINTING HISTORY

Macmillian edition published October 1985

Bantam Skylark edition / March 1987

ISBN 0-553-15484-2

Published simultaneously in the United States and Canada

PRINTED IN THE UNITED STATES OF AMERICA

S   0 9 8 7 6 5 4 3 2 1

To
Whit and Jamie
James and Clemmy
and all the little boys
and dogs
and
CATS
I have loved

BELLA ARABELLA

ONE

Arabella Fitzgerald, age ten, lived in a fantastically beautiful house set high on a hill above the Hudson River. It had been built in 1800 by her great-great-great-grandfather, old George Simon, who called the house Simon Hall. It had passed on to old George's son, also named George, then to his grandson George, his great-grandson George (who was the last George), and finally it had gone to that George's only child, his daughter, Diana. Diana was Arabella's mother.

With its soaring towers and battlements, its low balconies and deep terraces, and its rambling wings, Simon Hall was more like a castle than a mansion or a big house, and anyone who believed in castles and fairy tales loved Simon Hall.

Diana Simon had grown up, inherited the Hall, and married a man named Gerald Fitzgerald. Not long after, he died, leaving her a lonely and unhappy young widow with a small child. Soon she married again. In fact, she remarried three times, becoming Mrs. Center, Mrs. Myers, and now, as this story opens, Mrs. Tom Fales. She had been Mrs. Fales for a month.

Thus it seemed that the name of Simon had disappeared for good. But if you went down the long winding driveway beneath the canopy of interlacing locust trees to the main road, you would see that the name on the mailbox and the gate had stayed the same, just as the house had. Everyone loved the way old George had built Simon Hall and no one ever wanted to change anything.

Some said it was a house where time didn't want to move on, with the river running endlessly by, the same flowers blooming drowsily in the long formal gardens each season, the years bringing the same activities. Generations of old George's descendants remained, never wanting to leave home for very long. They just stayed and stayed and stayed. All but Arabella's mother, that is, as you will soon learn.

And then there were the cats that stayed, the cats of Simon Hall. Dogs had come and gone with generations of owners, and parakeets and parrots and goats and peacocks and horses and sheep. But there were always cats. Marmalade cats, calico cats, Persian cats, Siamese cats, Burmese cats, tabby cats, and alley cats. Oh, not all at once, mind you, but over the past hundred and twenty years there was one or another kind of cat, sometimes many, sometimes only one. Arabella, her mother, and her new stepfather were in the "only one" stage. This was a big handsome coal-black cat named Miranda.

Miranda had been there as long as Arabella could remember. She had come to Simon Hall as a very, very small kitten before Arabella was born, and sometimes even Arabella's mother couldn't remember the exact year she had come. "Miranda? Why, she's been here forever!" her mother would exclaim. That, of course, was not quite accurate, but it *had* been a very long time.

Arabella loved Miranda dearly and vice versa. Miranda slept on Arabella's bed, rubbed her leg, played ball-of-string with her, and followed her down to the river for walks. She sat on Arabella's lap and licked her fingers, and Arabella thought she was the most perfect cat in the whole wide world. In fact, she loved Miranda best of anyone in the entire world. Of course, she loved her mother very much; but after her father died, Arabella's mother and her new husbands were always too busy to pay much attention to her. They were away so much, leaving Simon Hall, returning, then going away again: to the city, to Europe, on trains, on ships, on strange safaris, and to remote resorts. So it was understandable that Arabella should care for Miranda more.

Arabella had tried to make them want to stay at home. She was adorably sweet to her stepfathers, thanking them prettily for the expensive toys they brought, always doing little things to make them feel permanent, like real fathers and not just temporary houseguests, as she could have treated them. She tried to call them "Daddy" or "Father" or even just "Dad"; but they always answered "Call me Frank" or "Bob" or whatever it was.

Now it was "Tom." When she had reached out and taken his hand and smiled and said, "Shall I call you Daddy?" he had replied, "Just call me Tom," patted her on the head, and gone on his way. She had wished that they would love her; but not one of them had. Not *really* loved her, the way she wanted to be loved. It made her sad, very sad. Sometimes she wasn't even sure that her mother really loved her. She was only sure that Miranda did.

"You always love me," Arabella said as she ran her fingers

down Miranda's soft nose. "I can tell by the way you lick my hands and purr so loud when I kiss you and scratch behind your ears. And if you don't stop squirming so much while I'm hugging you, I'll go off and leave you and then you can see how it feels." Poor little Arabella. But wasn't it lucky that she and Miranda had each other?

Her new stepfather, Tom Fales, barely spoke to her and so far had bought her only a few books (which she had already read, but would never have told him, instead thanking him profusely and telling him how much she liked them). She recognized the look of a traveler about him, and she sadly figured she wouldn't see too much of him—or her mother. Her mother was wild about Tom; she seemed to like him more than the last two. He talked a lot, calling everyone "darling," and told stories about all kinds of famous people whose names Arabella barely recognized. She certainly didn't understand the stories, but she thought he must be very clever and smart and was proud that he was her new stepfather. He had spent some years in Italy and was constantly using Italian words; he said *Ciao* to everyone in person or on the phone and answered with *Si* and called Arabella's mother *Cara mia*. He said *Grazie* when Mrs. Blackburn, the housekeeper, gave him the newspaper and *Prego* when Cook thanked him for telling her how delicious dinner was. Arabella was very impressed.

He was not at all like Arabella's real father, who had been big and strong and more handsome than anyone, and who had spoken in plain English. (He had been killed when she was very young and she didn't remember too awfully much about him, except that he came into her bedroom at night and kissed her and Miranda both and sang funny Irish songs that made them laugh and purr.)

When the new Mrs. Tom Fales had brought her husband
home for the first time, Arabella had clapped her hands
happily and run upstairs to put on the costume she wore at
dancing class. Then she had come down and perfectly per-
formed her best welcoming dance, which she thought he
surely would like to see. But instead he had only said, "Really, *cara mia*," and her mother had said, "That's nice, dear,
now run along." So she had run with Miranda to the bottom
of the garden and sat on the grass, where she got frightful
green grass stains on her ruffled net tutu and blinked in the
bright sunshine that made her eyes all watery and teary.

"We'll pick flowers for him, Miranda. Lots of people don't
like ballet, but everyone likes flowers. And we'll try to remember some funny story we've heard and tell it to him,
because we know he likes funny stories. That one Cook told

us about stuffing a pea might be good. Remember how everyone in the kitchen laughed? I'll have to ask her again to make sure I get it straight. We'd better do something in a hurry, or they'll get bored and be on the road again. I heard him say he liked new and different places. You know what that means."

But before they could do anything to win Tom over to them, Arabella's mother told her they were going to take a trip, a month-late honeymoon she called it. Though her mother said it would be for only a short while, Arabella felt that heart-wrenching moment of loneliness that dogs and cats feel when they get left behind, that timeless loneliness that stays the same whether a loved one is gone for a minute or a year. (Dogs and cats, you see, can't think in hours and days. Time is just one unending moment for them.) Of course, Arabella would not exactly be left by herself. She had Miranda, Mrs. Blackburn (who also had been at Simon Hall forever), Cook, the maid, the chauffeur, and the gardener. Still, it made her terribly said. She had been nice to Tom in every way she knew how. She had offered him a cooky when she was dying to eat it herself, and she had tried to keep her hands clean so that when she sat in the living room with Tom and her mother they wouldn't send her away to wash up. But it had all been useless; they were about to take off on a trip, without her. Her heart felt very heavy.

"Well, it will be all right, Miranda," she said, scooping up the big bundle of huggable black fur. "We've survived it all before. Anyway, while school's still in session, we really don't have time to do much else, especially with parents. They take up a lot of time. It'll be all right. You'll see." She buried her face in Miranda's side and choked back a sob.

TWO

Arabella went to a private day school nearby, but she was home by three o'clock and then she and Miranda did marvelous things together, like having milk and cookies in the kitchen with Cook, and helping the chauffeur polish the cars (Miranda loved to chase the polishing rag), and going down to the river to sail little berry-basket boats the gardener made for her. Arabella was happiest during these fun times, and all the servants were ever so nice to her.

The afternoon before her mother and Tom were to leave, Arabella skipped down the stairs from the third floor (where she and Miranda and Mrs. Blackburn had their rooms) and went to her mother's room to say good-bye, just in case they were going out for dinner and she wouldn't see them again. She had one hand on the doorknob and the other raised to knock, when she heard her name being spoken inside the room. Naturally curious, as all small girls are, she drew back her hands and leaned her ear nearer to the door to hear

what was being said. The voices were quite loud enough for her to hear clearly.

"Such a ridiculous thing to say, Tom, darling." Her mother's voice was high and melodious like a songbird's.

"Not at all. It can't possibly be healthy for a growing ten-year-old girl to live here alone."

"She's hardly alone. A great deal of money is paid out to have people in the house. She has Mrs. Blackburn, my very own Mrs. Blackburn, whose mother and grandmother were with us, Cook, and the maid . . ."

"Servants. Servants, darling, dearest, *cara mia*, all servants. And servants do not take the place of family and friends. Even five servants."

"Mrs. Blackburn," her mother replied sweetly, "Mrs. Blackburn is a saint and an absolute angel to her. She's been with us for years, since long before Arabella was born. She's as much a part of the house as all the Georges. She's like one of the family. Of course the child has a friend."

"She hasn't had a playmate here since I've been around." Tom spoke authoritatively. "It's plain to see she is starved for affection."

"You've only been here a month," her mother reminded him.

"Si, si. But I have eyes. She is alone every afternoon. True, I am not accustomed to children, having never had any of my own, but even I can see that she is lonely. Darling Diana, answer me honestly: Does she see little friends?"

"Of course. Every day at school. And many times they come home with her. Many times. I can't remember exactly when she had one last, but it's happened many times. Besides, she seems perfectly adjusted and happy being alone."

"There! That's it! Even you admit she's alone. 'Happy being alone.' Nonsense. No child prefers being alone. She is unhappy here. I would spend more time with her myself, but I don't know how to entertain her." There was a long pause. "My dearest, I can see that I'm going to have to be very firm with you. You need someone to guide you."

Arabella's mother quickly responded. "Do you really think so?"

"Definitely. And there are some things you will just have to take my word for. If you love me, you will."

"You know I love you." She spoke the words softly.

"Then, for her own good, Arabella must be sent away to

school. I absolutely insist. It's for her own good," he repeated. "She needs more than she is getting. I worry about
her."

"She's such a baby still."

"She's too old to be a baby," he said with exasperation.
"She acts like one because she's starved for attention and
friends. She's ten years old and acts like she's six. We must
help her," he stated in a very determined manner. "It's not
healthy for her to be here alone so much." He lowered his
voice and spoke soothingly. "*Cara mia,* she needs compan-
ionship. Think of the child. Think of her loneliness."

"Do you really think it would be best?" Her mother's
voice took on that softened, giving-in tone that revealed the
bending of a will.

"Positively. It would be best for *her.* Surely you understand
what I am saying."

"What will she say?"

"She'll love it. Take my word for it. She'll love it. I will
speak to her for you. I know just how to approach her. It will
be like going on a long trip, an adventure, with lots of
wonderful playmates. She will be deliriously happy. *Positivo.*"

"Oh, darling Tom, of course you're right. You're always
right. It will be for the best." She paused. "Best for Arabella.
We'll tell her together."

That was all Arabella heard. She turned and ran as fast as
she could down the hall, up the stairs, down the next hall,
and into her room. She slammed the door shut, then burst
into tears and threw herself across the bed, her thick brown
hair tumbling across her head like a hood.

"He hates me, he hates me, he hates me," she sobbed into
the quilt that lay folded across the foot of the bed. "He's
sending me away, away from my own home, from my friends,

from my beloved everything—oh, Miranda." The black cat jumped on the bed and rubbed against the little shaking shoulder. "Oh, Miranda, he's sending me away from you. I can't go. I can't. I can't. My poor heart will break." She sobbed even louder. It was a wonder the whole household didn't rush upstairs to find out what was wrong. But only Miranda could hear the pitiful wailing. Gently, she continued to rub her cheeks against Arabella's trembling body. "I tried to make him love me, but he just ended up hating me. Why did Mother listen to him? Why? What does he know? He's so new!" She choked and gasped. "I'll run away or die first. That's it. I'll die first. Maybe I'm dying now. I hope so. I wish I were dead." She cried and pounded her fists on the bed for a long time before she spoke again. "Oh, dearest Miranda, if only I were a cat, then I could stay. All the cats here are loved and wanted. But I'm only a poor little girl and unless I die I'll have to go. I'll die right away."

"Nonsense," a voice said.

Arabella gasped and held her breath. She hadn't known anyone was in the room with her. She quickly sat up and looked around the room. There were dolls and toys and games, stuffed animals and skis and tennis rackets, sofas and chairs and tables (it was a very big room), but nothing—and no one—else.

"Miranda," she whispered. "Did you hear someone speak?"

"Of course, silly."

Arabella's eyes grew bigger and bluer than they had ever been before. She slowly turned her head and looked at the cat. They stared and stared at each other, one with eyes as big as playhouse saucers and one through narrow slits of yellow.

The little girl put her hand to her mouth and whispered through her fingers. "I must be very sick, delirious, already dying. I thought I heard a voice, but there's only you, and you can't talk."

"Can't I?"

Arabella jumped back and huddled against the head of the bed, her thick brown hair falling across her face.

"Don't be a ninny, child; I'm still the same old me. I'm not going to bite. Just because I can talk doesn't mean I'm dangerous." Miranda purred loudly and swished her tail, the whole thing, not just the tip the way she did when she was dreaming.

"Cats can't talk! No cat can talk!" Arabella sniffed loudly and wiped her hand across her nose.

"You're wrong there, my love. All cats can talk. It's only that so few people can hear us. It takes a certain type of cat-person, a very special cat-person, to know this. There hasn't been one in your family for a long, long time. The first wife of the second George—George, Jr.—was one. That was your great-great grandmother. Your grandfather George came very close, but never quite made it all the way across. Poor man, he just thought he was going mad and finally locked himself in the north tower. Then he really did go mad and when he came out it was feet first. It was very sad. Such a sweet man. A gentle loony. But a real loony at the end." She uncrooked her right back knee and stuck her leg straight out, then began to lick her thigh.

"How do you know all that? Those people lived hundreds of years ago." Arabella said "hundreds" the way people do when they mean anything more than five years ago.

"We cats always pass along historical information about our house families. We never fail to report every detail to the next one who comes. That's how legends are kept alive. Gray Stranger, the cat your grandmother brought in during a storm, had a wonderful memory and a real knack for telling a tale. He could sit all night by the fire, that slate-gray coat turning pink with the flames, and keep all the cats spellbound the whole night. Then they'd all sleep the entire next day. The mouse population quadrupled during his reign. He lived to be very old. Striped Abigail got everything from Gray Stranger, and then she told me before she passed away. She forgot a few things, but I got them from Thompson, a wonderful Manx who was before your memory. You were not yet two when he died."

"I remember him. He used to beat up all the cats in the neighborhood."

"You remember hearing about him. But that's the one. He was a good storyteller, too."

"Amazing." Arabella slid down the crocheted coverlet toward the foot of the bed.

"Yes." Miranda now licked one elegant front paw, sending out her claws and briefly inspecting them.

"What will I do, Miranda? If I don't die, I'll be sent away. And that would be worse than death. Even running away would be terrible, because I'd have to leave here. And I don't really want to lock myself in the north tower and go mad. Oh, if only they loved me, how simple it would be."

"What would you like to do?" Miranda raised her head and narrowed her eyes to peer at Arabella.

"Why," Arabella cocked her head sideways, "I think I'd like to become a cat, a cat just like you. I'd like to be one of the cats of Simon Hall. They're never sent away. They get to stay on and on forever, and people love them dearly."

Miranda looked at her a long, long time, then stood up and arched her back, stretching out her front legs and extending her claws. Arabella copied her by putting her arms way out in front of her and wiggling her fingers; she pulled up her shoulders the way Miranda did and felt a delicious tingling down her spine.

Finally Miranda sat back down and quietly asked, "Would you really? I mean, think, child. Would you really—really and truly—like to be a cat?"

Arabella thought it over very carefully. "Yes," she answered. "Yes, I really and truly would. Don't you believe me?"

"I suppose a ten-year-old knows her mind. You certainly know you don't want to leave this house."

"Can I become one? I mean, is it actually possible?" It sounded positively *impossible*, but then, so did talking cats.

"Yes. Many things are possible." Miranda looked very wise. Arabella thought she was the wisest-looking creature she had ever seen.

"But how?" she asked.

"Well," said Miranda in a very confidential tone, "you have to be a real cat-person to start with. . . ."

"Which you said I was."

"Yes. Then you have to want it with all your heart."

"Which I do."

"Only your heart knows that. You may just be talking with your head."

"I think I know what my heart wants."

"Yes, I believe you do."

"I know I would be happy. All the cats who have ever lived here have been happy, or," she paused, reaching back to scratch the base of her spine, "I hope they have."

"Oh, yes, they have been. Not one has ever complained. Even Freddy-Cat Johnson, who was a born complainer and got thrown out of the Johnsons' house because of it, even he loved it here."

"Then I do want it. Please, Miranda." Arabella put her face close to Miranda's. "Please tell me what to do to become a cat."

"But, silly," Miranda said, rubbing her cheek against Arabella's, "you already are one."

THREE

Arabella froze and stared at Miranda, whose words were ringing in her ears. She was afraid to move, knowing instinctively that Miranda never told a lie or even said anything unnecessary. She tried to sit as motionless as a statue, but her eyes involuntarily looked down at her hand lying across Miranda's paw. For an instant she stopped breathing. Her fingers had grown together into a slender round shape, and all the way up her forearm dark brown fur covered her skin. She gasped, jumped off the bed, and ran to the long mirror. Unbelievable. There in front of her stood a beautiful chocolate brown cat, just the color of Arabella's hair, with eyes as blue as Arabella's.

"Miranda! Miranda! Look!" the brown cat exclaimed in amazement. "Is that really me?!"

Miranda smiled indulgently. "That's really you. I knew with that hair of yours you'd make a fabulous cat." She lightly hopped down and sauntered to the mirror. "You're smaller than I, of course, and a little thin," she said, poking

Arabella in the ribs, "but with some of Cook's delicious cream and fish cakes you'll . . ."

"Fish cakes! I hate fish cakes! I hate all that fish stuff. And Cook knows it. She never gives me anything fishy."

"You mean you used," Miranda paused for emphasis, "to hate fish. You won't anymore. Cats love fish. It's part of being a cat. Even finicky eaters, like the first Mrs. George's precious Blue, eat fish. Speaking of that, let's go to the kitchen and look hungry."

Arabella could hardly tear herself away from the mirror. She looked at herself frontways and sideways; she looked down at her front legs and back at her tail, practicing swinging it back and forth. ("What fun!") She stretched, stuck out her claws ("Whee!"), and arched her back. She stepped close to the mirror, then backed up. From the tip of her small pointed nose, past the ears delicately placed just above the ruff at her neck, all the way to her tail as finely pointed as a sable watercolor brush, her fur lay more majestically than a mantle of mink.

"I'm almost as beautiful as you, Miranda . . . but not quite. I'll never be *that* beautiful."

Miranda purred loudly. "Now stop admiring yourself, my dear, and let's go see Cook."

Arabella gave one final toss of her head at the mirror, then ran to the door and reached up her paw. "Miranda," she wailed, "how will we get out? I can't even *begin* to reach the doorknob!" She meowed pitifully.

"Hush, hush. You must stop that little-girl wailing and whining. We'll get out the way I come in: through the window."

"The window? This is the third floor!"

"I am well aware of that. Calm down. There's a nice ledge to walk on to the corner of the house; then there's a stout vine that leads right down to the kitchen door. Simple as pie. Luckily Mrs. Blackburn believes in fresh air in the nursery and your window is always left open a few inches, summer or winter. Come along."

Miranda jumped lightly onto the sill and slid under the window. Arabella did the same.

"Oh, oh, it's so far down. It's farther than it used to be."

"No, it's only that you are smaller. Now follow me along this ledge."

"I'll fall."

"Silly. You won't fall. Cats are very nimble-footed."

"I've always been good at climbing trees," Arabella tried not to look down, "and climbing on top of the gardener's shed," it almost made her sick to look straight ahead, "and I didn't get scared that time I went on the Ferris wheel with the stepfather before Tom—" she halted. "I can't remember his name."

"Bob. You're doing fine; keep moving."

"Oh, yes, Bob. He was nice. I liked him quite a bit, but I don't think he much liked me. Remember when he brought us the ice cream? Peppermint. It was our favorite and it was his favorite, too. I thought he'd really love us after he found that out. Remember, Miranda, how he brought it home for us? Is it much farther?"

"No. Here's the vine now. Just jump onto it and climb down."

"Head first?"

"If you prefer. I like backing down and seeing where I've been."

"I'm scared. Suppose I fall?"

"You won't. That's why you have those claws." Miranda spoke kindly. "You'll do just fine."

"Miranda, I do love you. You're such a comfort to me. If I don't make it, remember that." Arabella trembled as she looked at the vine. "It doesn't look very stout to me."

"It's very strong; and it's grown right into the stones of the house. It won't come loose and you won't fall. Just hold onto it and climb down." And away Miranda went, jumping gracefully onto the vine and disappearing down it as smoothly as a raindrop sliding down a spout.

"Wait for me!" Arabella cried out. "Please! Don't leave me here alone! Not on my very first climb! Wait! Wait!" She meowed loudly and threw herself onto the vine and without thinking hurried after Miranda. The next thing she knew her back feet touched the ground. She hadn't even noticed whether she had gone down feet first or head first. "Glorious!" she cried out, looking at the sky where the vine reached endlessly upward. "That's some climb. But it was easy, easy as pie."

Miranda smiled and purred proudly. "I told you it would be. Come on." She led Arabella to the kitchen door and scratched gently. "If that doesn't work, I meow."

"What if that doesn't work?"

"Then I yowl and throw myself against the door. Someone always responds to that. Look smart now; here comes someone."

The door opened and there stood Cook, looming above them like a towering giant. "It's you, is it, Miranda? And look here, will you. You've brought a friend."

Miranda swished her tail and walked past Cook into the warm kitchen, which smelled of freshly baked sweet buns.

Arabella stayed planted on the steps. She couldn't get over the size of Cook! She had always thought Cook was an ordinary person, but suddenly she had become this unbelievable giant.

Miranda stopped and looked back. "Come on in."

Arabella meowed softly. "She's so huge."

Miranda laughed. "It's the first human you've seen since you changed over. You'll get used to it. It's a shock at first, though, I'm sure."

Cook swooped down and stroked Arabella's head. "What a lovely brown kitty you've brought home, Miranda. Where did you find her?"

Miranda winked at Arabella. "Wouldn't she be surprised if she knew. Come in, child. No one will hurt you."

Arabella was afraid, in spite of the friendly greeting from Cook. Everything seemed so strange. She looked from Cook to Miranda and back again. She didn't know what to do.

Cook stepped aside. "Do come in, sweet brown kitty. Any friend of Miranda's is most welcome."

That was nice. Arabella always had liked Cook, and now more than ever. She felt good all over. She looked back at her tail and gave it a practice swing, so she would be able to do it with style when she entered, just the way Miranda had. She held her head high, swished her tail, and walked confidently past Cook to stand next to Miranda. She glanced over her shoulder and admired her tail. How perfectly she had made her entrance. And Cook hadn't shut her tail in the door, even though it was so long.

Miranda purred and rubbed her cheek against Arabella. "See how nice it is? Your first big step as a cat into the world of humans. Now look hungry."

Cook poured cream into two dishes and put them side by side on the floor. Then she cut up a chicken liver and put it on a little china plate between the dishes of cream. "There you are, Miranda; I hope your friend likes liver too."

"I hate it. She knows I hate it." Arabella stuck her muzzle into the cool sweet cream and lapped with her tongue. She looked up, dripping the frothy white liquid from her chin. "This is good. I'm only going to eat this. I hate liver and I hate fish."

"You'll like the chicken liver; try it." Miranda munched on a piece. "It's quite delicious. Tender and fresh. On Fridays she gives me a juicy lamb kidney fresh from the butcher's weekend delivery. Now, that's something really good."

"Yuck! It sounds repulsive." She sniffed the liver and turned away. "I'll stick to the cream, thank you. I wish she'd give us one of those sweet buns with lots of butter on it."

Miranda smiled. "You wouldn't care for it much anymore; sweet rolls are for little girls. Though Striped Abigail liked that sort of thing. She was fat as a pig, too. Her two front legs stuck out, then the rest of her kind of swelled out in a great mass that ended in her tail. Your chin's a mess. Try not to put your whole face in the bowl. Just the tongue."

Arabella looked at her in surprise.

"Never mind, you'll soon get the hang of it." She daintily ate the last piece of liver.

Arabella thought Miranda also rather swelled out in a great mass that ended in her tail, but she wouldn't have told her and hurt her feelings for the world.

Cook reached down and removed the plate. "Now, Miranda, you and the little brown beauty move over to the window and have a nap. I've got to attend to the cooking. I want to send one of these buns up to Arabella to hold her until dinner. As soon as Mrs. Blackburn's finished her tea, she can take it up." Cook talked a lot. "Madam has decided to stay in tonight, and she wants to have Arabella's favorite chicken croquettes for dinner, it being their last night before Madam goes away," Cook shook her head, "and I've got to get on with this bird. Take that last lick of cream, kitty. There you are—now off with you."

"I'm not accustomed to napping at this time of day," Arabella whispered to Miranda.

"I know that, but come sit in the sun with me anyway. It feels glorious on your back." Miranda went to a big shelf in the pantry and jumped into the stream of sunlight.

Arabella followed. "What a nice place. You're all to yourself here, and right next to the cooky jar."

Miranda was purring loudly and seemed not to hear her.

"You know what, Miranda? This is all ever so nice—so far. And isn't Cook sweet to think of sending me a bun to tide me over? She does that lots, you know. I just love Cook. Next to Mrs. Blackburn, she's about my best friend. . . ." She caught herself quickly. "Human, that is. I've always loved you the best of all." She looked at Miranda, who was sitting with her neatly rounded front feet close together, licking her upper leg in rhythm with her vibrant purring. Her black fur glistened in the pink and gold rays of the setting sun.

"There are so many things I'll have to learn." Arabella opened her eyes very wide and sat quite still. "For instance, how will I know when I've grown up? Little girls know because they start a new grade in school every year and can't fit into their last year's clothes anymore. But how will I know now? I'll have the same clothes forever and I won't go to school. How will I know when I grow up, Miranda?"

Miranda stopped licking and looked at Arabella, barely able to focus her eyes. "You won't need to know. Human time will become unimportant to you. One day you will only remember that you once were smaller and played chase with your tail, but that will seem very far off. Time means nothing; we don't think of yesterdays and tomorrows. Only todays matter." She closed her eyes.

"I will get bigger, won't I?"

"Hmmmmm."

"Today is nice. The next today will be nice, too, won't it?"

"Hmmmmm."

"You will have to stay near me and tell me what to do. You will, won't you?"

Shadows crept slowly into the pantry.

"Miranda? Miranda? Are you asleep?"

Arabella put her head quite close to Miranda.

"Just listen to you." Arabella cocked her head. "How do you make so much noise?" Suddenly her eyes grew very large and round, the blue centers rimmed with light brown. "In fact, how do you make *that* sound at all? I mean, how do you purr? I haven't done that yet and you haven't said anything about it. Miranda. Are you listening?"

"What?" She raised her black head and stared with narrowed eyes that clearly indicated she didn't want to be disturbed.

"I said, how do you purr?"

"Later, child, later. I'm relaxing now. I do not like to be disturbed when I am trying to relax."

Arabella lay down next to Miranda and tried to think about purring, but the cream in her stomach and the warm sun on her back blurred her thinking and she began to feel very sleepy. Her eyelids closed and her head drooped to the shelf as she sank into slumber.

FOUR

Arabella was suddenly awakened by a great deal of loud talking and shouting.

"Where did you look?" Cook shouted out the back door.

A voice Arabella recognized as the gardener's answered, "All over! I even went down to the river. And along the shore. She's just not anywhere!" He came and stood just inside the back door. "She's not anywhere."

"She has to be somewhere! Who saw her last?"

Silence followed as Cook, Mrs. Blackburn, and the gardener all looked suspiciously at each other. Suddenly Cook said "It was you!" and whirled toward the chauffeur, who was standing by the pantry looking terrified.

"No, no. I brought her home from school as I always do." He stepped back. "I never saw her again. She went into the house, and I never saw her again. Never. Just home from school and not again."

"We'll have to tell Mrs. . . ." Mrs. Blackburn couldn't remember Arabella's mother's latest name, "Madam."

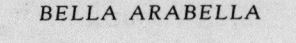

"Yes," Cook agreed. "You'd better."

Mrs. Blackburn stared at the others. "Maybe we should search once more."

"That's right," they all said eagerly.

"Once more." Cook spoke quietly. "No point in upsetting Madam if she's hiding someplace around here."

"She never hides," said Mrs. Blackburn. "She's simply someplace where we haven't looked."

They all scattered from the room, two searching inside the house and two outside.

An hour later, they met again in the kitchen, with the maid in tow. The five of them were in obvious distress;

anxiety was written on their faces. No one spoke for a long time.

Finally Mrs. Blackburn said in a tense, low voice, "There's nothing for it but to tell Madam and call the police."

They all sucked in their breath and solemnly nodded agreement.

It took Arabella quite a long time after the commotion woke her to figure out what was going on. She sat up and blinked several times and listened carefully. When she realized it was about *her*, she jumped a foot and meowed loudly. "Miranda! Miranda! Wake up! They think I'm gone! Miranda!"

This startled Miranda so much she almost fell off the shelf. "Child! Don't shout so. Calm yourself and speak slowly." She looked around at the nervous congregation. "What on earth is going on?"

"It's me!" She lowered her voice. "It's me. They think I'm missing and they're calling the police."

"It was bound to happen."

"I'm here! I'm here! Oh, Miranda, they can't hear me. I'm here! Miranda, do something! Tell them!" she cried.

"Slow down. Just slow down. Any wailing from us will just get us put out and we'll never know what's going on. Now keep quiet and let's listen."

The two of them sat very attentively, side by side on the pantry shelf, and listened, and learned.

"What shall we do?" Arabella whimpered.

Miranda covered the new little cat's paw comfortingly with her own and answered simply, "Nothing. There's no way to tell them you're here, because none of them is a cat-person. There's nothing we can do. Now don't start crying again. I don't want to be put out, and it won't do any good at all. Just be brave. You'll see. Everything will be all right in time. Be brave and patient and trust me."

"Oh, Miranda, you know so much. What would I do without you? You're absolutely right. I'll just sit here and wait bravely. I won't even say they deserve it."

Miranda shot her an indignant look. "I should hope not."

The rest of the afternoon—in fact, much of the night— was filled with searching police lights and uniformed men, men with dogs (who were terrifying even to look at) and men with sticks, poking under the bushes. The sounds of authoritative voices cracked back and forth in the darkness, while babbling confusion filled the many-roomed mansion. Everyone had a guess as to where a lost little girl might be lost; but no one could find her.

Arabella's mother had prostrated herself on her bedroom chaise, weeping into a succession of embroidered handkerchiefs, faintly offering an occasional suggestion of where to search. With each negative report, she wept and cried out in a pitiful manner and fluttered her diamond-studded fingers in a gesture of dismissal.

Arabella's stepfather chain-smoked and paced the long downstairs hall filled with portraits of the Georges, nervously casting an occasional glance at the staring ancestral eyes as they followed him back and forth.

In the kitchen Mrs. Blackburn sat, pale and thin-lipped, in a straight-backed chair, saying nothing as she blinked away tears. She didn't even notice when the new brown cat jumped onto her lap and looked at her lovingly.

Cook bustled about, trying to keep busy and not cry, shaping minced chicken into small neat croquettes, mixing up a batch of chocolate drop cooky dough, sharpening knives, peeling potatoes. She bit her lip and shook her head vigorously every two minutes. This too helped her not to cry.

The maid, however, was making a fool of herself, whimpering and sniffling and whining about why weren't they looking in this place or that, when everyone knew these places had been searched at least ten times. Mrs. Blackburn and Cook tried to ignore her; it wasn't easy.

Arabella sat with confused emotions on Mrs. Blackburn's lap, just the way she had when she was a very little girl. She thought her mother and Tom deserved to be unhappy, but not the others. She wanted to say something to Mrs. Blackburn, to purr some comfort to her, to reassure her and show that she loved her. Purr? She raised her head. She hadn't yet done that. She didn't even know how to start.

On and on and on, for days that lasted ever so long it seemed, the search continued. Arabella's mother drifted from her bedroom to the terrace and back again, clutching handkerchiefs and finally carrying a box of tissues. Tom Fales smoked a lot and drank a lot, and tried to console his wife with sweet words and frequent hugs. Newspaper reporters came, and strangers from up and down the river stared curiously and offered advice. Buildings were searched, repeatedly, lawns and gardens trampled, furniture overturned. Still nothing, no sign, no clue was found. The officials sadly shook their heads and said they would stay on the case; then they went away.

Throughout this turmoil, Arabella alternated between listening and wailing loudly. While secretly she relished the excitement (though she was careful not to tell Miranda, who wouldn't approve), later it made her cry. "Even if they did want to send me away, I still love them. Oh, Miranda, can't you tell them I'm here? Poor Mrs. Blackburn, I never knew she could be sad. She's always been so cheerful. And Cook, dear Cook, she even burned the tea cakes. My mother seems so unhappy, and so does Tom. I think they're really worried."

Miranda did what she could to quiet Arabella. "Hush, now, hush. Come and eat some nice tuna and calm down."

"Tuna! I hate fish!"

"Try it." Miranda daintily ate small pieces and purred loudly. "Delicious."

"I won't. I won't eat fish of any kind. Not tuna fish or liver or raw eggs or any of those horrible things you eat."

"You don't know what you're missing. You can't live on cream alone."

"I wish my mother wouldn't cry so much."

"She'll stop soon."

"Will she? That would be nice. It really upsets me to see her cry. Maybe she does deserve it, for agreeing to send me away. But," she hastened to add, "I still don't like to see her cry. She must really love me. Do you think she loves me?" Before Miranda could reply, Arabella asked plaintively, "Do you think Tom hates me?"

"No."

"I think he must. He wants to send me away."

"Nonsense."

"Nonsense? You're not always right, you know."

Miranda didn't dignify this with an answer. Arabella felt a twitch of shame for having said it. The smell of fish was very strong. She blinked a few times to fight back her tears. She wasn't sure whether it was the fish or sadness that was making her cry.

"Miranda," she ventured softly, "maybe, just maybe I've made a mistake."

Miranda paused in mid-bite and shifted her eyes sideways to look at her. "What do you mean?"

"Well, I mean, maybe I should have stayed a little girl."

"You may recall that you were miserably unhappy then."

"I do recall that. But look at all the trouble I've caused this way. I feel awful about it."

"That's true. But do you think reappearing as a little girl would solve your problems? It would solve theirs, but not yours. As soon as they knew you were safe, you'd be packed off to school."

"They wouldn't do that *now*. They'd be so happy to see me they'd never send me away."

"Foolish one. You'd be sent away faster than before, to keep you safe and prevent your vanishing again."

"But if they did, I could just become a cat again. Couldn't I?"

"No. There's no such thing as becoming a cat 'again.' Once a cat, always a cat."

"What do you mean?"

"Just that."

"Always a cat? Can't I become a little girl again?"

"No."

"*No?*"

"No." Miranda walked past her and leapt onto a kitchen chair. "No, I'm afraid not. Just accept things as they are and try to make the most of them." She curled her paws under her chest and let her head droop, purring softly, her tail swinging gracefully over the edge of the chair.

"I don't know if I can." Arabella looked to make sure Miranda was asleep, then she silently ran from the kitchen, through the pantry, into the long hall, and up the stairs. She stopped at her mother's door and looked in, past the narrow opening where the door had been pushed almost shut. Then she quietly slipped through, barely brushing her sides against the door jamb. She just had to let her mother know she was here and safe.

FIVE

*H*er mother was stretched out on the bed, one arm across her forehead, the other hanging limply over the side. A white cloth covered her eyes. Her stepfather's back was thin and sagged forward as he stared out the window.

Arabella sat down and looked from one to the other. She knew her mother loved her. What a comfort it would be if she just walked over and said "I'm here, Mother! I haven't gone away." She stepped gingerly across the thick carpet to the side of the bed and rubbed her head against her mother's hand.

The movement made her mother stir. She took the cloth from her eyes and cried softly: "Oh, Tom, what will I do?" Her fingers ran up and down the brown fur.

Tom quickly went to the side of the bed. With his foot he pushed Arabella aside and took the limp hand in his own. "My dearest. She will come back. Or she will be found. Both of us must be patient. I never knew I could feel such sadness."

Her mother sobbed. Tom sat down beside his wife and tried to soothe her.

Arabella felt very sad watching her mother. She jumped up on the bed, but was quickly put back on the floor by Tom. "Stay down, kitty," he said.

Arabella began to rub against his leg, hoping he would take a good look at her and recognize her. She rubbed as strongly as she could, pushing her head into his calf. If she could get him to look, if she could get him to lift her onto the bed and into her mother's arms, then they would see who she was and they would be happy. But he only pushed her away, saying, "Not now. Go away, kitty. Go on, out with you."

Arabella rubbed some more, this time meowing loudly. She tried to jump onto the bed again, but Tom caught her. Picking her up with one hand, he walked to the door, dropped her in the hall, and shut the door behind her.

Arabella wailed loudly, but to no avail. Sadly she padded along the hall and went up the stairs to her own room. It was exactly the same as if she had just come home from school. Her dolls, the tea set, the books and games, all were ready and waiting to her to come back. The window was opened enough for Miranda to come in and out, just as always. The pink and green quilt was folded at the foot of her bed, just as always. She sat down and looked around, sad that no one knew she was here, but glad nothing had been changed. She had no idea how long she had been a cat, but it seemed a very long time. She hoped no one would ever change anything or forget her. She knew Mrs. Blackburn loved her very much. If only Tom loved her and hadn't wanted to send her away, how happy they would all be now. But he didn't love her.

Arabella went downstairs to the kitchen. Everything seemed unchanged here, too, with Cook at the stove and Miranda on the chair asleep. Arabella ambled absently to the dish of food on the floor and took a bite. Maybe it would have been better to have gone away to boarding school; at least everyone wouldn't be crying. However, this way she was here, at home, with her own room, with everyone she loved, with Miranda. She took another bite. She had never had this kind of food before. She touched it with her paw and then licked it. Tuna fish! Well, imagine that. Not as bad as she thought it would be. She glanced over her shoulder to make sure Miranda wasn't watching, then took a few more bites. Licking her face clean, she sprang up beside Miranda and put her head close to the thick black fur.

"How do you do that?"

"What?" Miranda asked grumpily.

"That. Purr."

Miranda yawned and shut her eyes again. "Don't bother me now, child. I'm very sleepy."

"You're always asleep. How can you sleep so much? Have you always? I never noticed."

There was no answer—only the lulling purr of contentment.

The morning sun warmed the earth, dispersing the last of winter's gloom. Green daffodil shoots were spearing upward seeking the sun. Migrating birds were twittering among tiny pink buds and green buds, gaily dancing with a joyous air. Mrs. Blackburn opened more windows, hoping some of the sadness that filled the house would float away and that renewed spirits might stream in with the light. She and Cook both kept busy and tried to run things in a reasonably normal fashion, but often they wept for their lost little girl.

Tom had persuaded Arabella's mother to join him on the terrace. She sat listlessly, a broad-brimmed hat protecting her fair face from the sun. Tom sat next to her and held her pale, thin hand. He had been very attentive to her during this terrible time, saying soft words to cheer her and touching her with frequent loving gestures. She smiled wanly behind the thin handkerchief she held over her tear-reddened eyes.

Arabella and Miranda sat on the low stone wall that enclosed the terrace. While Miranda watched the birds, clearly fascinated by the busy little creatures, muttering "enticing" and working her tail, Arabella sadly watched her mother and Tom, trying to think of a way to reassure them, her mother especially. It was a very sad time indeed.

The police did stay on the case. A nice big man in a blue uniform came to the house and looked for clues, searching from the cavernous rooms of the cellar to the tall stone towers, from the bushes by the garages all the way to the willows that trailed their leafy branches in the river's flow. He was now a regular sight in the household.

"Terrible," he had said to Arabella's mother more than once, hanging his head and staring at the floor. "I have little ones of my own and I can imagine what it's like for you. But we'll find her. I won't stop until she's found."

Arabella's mother always cried aloud when he said this and dropped to the nearest chair, waving him away with one pale hand while she pressed the back of the other to her brow. Tom would blink in a manly fashion, shake the policeman's hand, and thank him.

Mrs. Blackburn gave him coffee when he came in the morning and tea when he came in the afternoon. "Here you are, Policeman Barnes. And Cook made this for you." There would be thick slices of hot homemade bread, with melting butter and raspberry jam, or muffins right from the oven, dripping honey onto the fragile little plate he balanced on his big palm. "You must keep up your strength," she would say, fighting back tears. "You mustn't fail us."

"There, there. Try not to worry so much. I know I'll find her."

But, in fact, it was not Policeman Barnes who found Arabella; it was quite the other way around.

He was sitting at the kitchen table having a last cup of tea before going home when Arabella jumped right onto his lap. It finally occurred to her that maybe, just maybe, he was a cat-person and would be able to understand her. She put her face very close to his and meowed as loudly as she could, staring into his eyes for a sign of recognition.

"What's this?" he cried, pushing aside his cup. "It's a little kitty. What's its name?" he asked Mrs. Blackburn.

"Oh, that one." Mrs. Blackburn reached across the table and patted Arabella. "We don't know. She just walked in with Miranda. We have no idea who owns her and in the turmoil no one's paid much attention to her."

"A stray?" He smiled at Arabella and scratched her under the chin. "Pretty little thing."

Arabella sat down on his lap in disgust. She did not want her chin scratched. She wanted to be recognized. She spied the pitcher of milk that sat next to the empty tea cup and, putting one paw on the table, stood and stretched her chin toward the white liquid.

"Hold on!" Policeman Barnes pulled her back onto his lap. "In my house you wouldn't be allowed to do that, and I don't think you should do it here." He looked thoughtfully at her. "My little ones sure would enjoy a kitty like you." He looked at Mrs. Blackburn. "Nothing in the lost-and-found column about her?"

"Nothing. I've looked several times. No description is even close to her. I suppose she'll just settle in here and become one of the cats of Simon Hall. We've had so many over the years. In my time alone, there have been dozens, too many to count. And there are many stories about them, some of which are very strange. I am one of the few who remember them. But everyone knows about the cats of Simon Hall. They're quite famous, you know."

"I don't suppose you'd let me have her, would you? To take home to my children? They sure would like to have her," he said.

Arabella sat up with a start. The man must be mad, to think anyone would allow her to leave Simon Hall. No cat had ever been turned away.

"Well, I don't know." Mrs. Blackburn pursed her lips and a crease developed between her eyes as she frowned. "On the one hand, she is very new, and I doubt if Madam has even seen her, so she doesn't really belong here. On the other hand, we have never had one quite that color, and she did come to the door of her own free will. I'm not sure." She turned to Cook. "What do you think?"

"You decide. My mind is so filled with . . . everything. . . ." She shook her head and punched down the dough. "I haven't had time to think about the new cat at all."

Policeman Barnes sat up very straight and leaned toward Mrs. Blackburn. "My children have never had a pet at all. We never thought we could afford one. But now I'm doing a little better, and we would be able to take care of it. What do you say?"

"Never a pet at all!" Cook cried. "The poor little tykes!"

"Oh." Mrs. Blackburn again reached over and patted Arabella. "If that's the case, it would be selfish of us to keep her. You take her, by all means, if it will bring happiness to your children."

"And you take these cinnamon buns to them," Cook said, bundling up a large package.

Arabella's heart began to race and she tried to jump down, but the policeman put his big hand under her middle and held her like a furry rag. He stood up. "Can you let me have a brown grocery bag? I've had to return stray cats to owners before, and I've found that putting them in a bag or a sack or even a pillowcase has a soothing effect on them."

Arabella wailed, dangling helplessly in the air, her feet wildly reaching out and touching nothing. "Miranda! Miranda!"

"She doesn't much like that position," Cook said, holding open the bag. "Let's get her in here and maybe she'll quiet down."

"Miranda! Miranda! Help! Help!"

Miranda reached the kitchen just in time to see Arabella being lowered into the bag. "Stop! Stop!" she shouted.

The policeman carefully folded over the top of the bag. "There. She'll calm down and stop crying. I can't wait to see the expressions on the children's faces when I open this."

Miranda stood on her hind legs and reached as high as she could, her paw tip just touching the bottom of the bag. "Arabella!"

The smothered sound of crying filled the kitchen. "Help! Miranda, help!"

Miranda stretched higher and higher, her shoulder aching with the strain, again touching the bag.

"Do something, Miranda! Do something!" the muffled voice wailed.

"Don't take her!" Miranda meowed desperately. "Don't! It's Arabella!" She looked frantically from Cook to Mrs. Blackburn. "It's Arabella!" she cried again, but to no avail.

"Thank you for the tea and the buns," Policeman Barnes said, going to the back door, carrying his two bags and smiling happily. "I'll be back tomorrow."

Miranda raced after him, batting the grocery bag, trying to take it from him. "Arabella! I'll follow you! I'll follow you all the way!"

Mrs. Blackburn reached down and picked up Miranda. "It's all right, Miranda. Calm down." She stroked the black fur. "Do you live far?" she asked him.

"Just north of here. Don't worry. As soon as I get her in the bicycle basket she'll quiet down. Thanks again, and good night."

The door shut on the wailing and screaming that came from the bag.

"Oh, my," Mrs. Blackburn said, still holding Miranda, who was struggling to get away. "Calm down, Miranda. I do hope we did the right thing," she said to Cook.

"It was a terrible scene, if you ask me," Cook said. "But it's done now. We'd both better have a cup of tea."

"Yes." Mrs. Blackburn sat down at the table. "I've never seen Miranda so agitated. And just feel her heart beating! Never anything like it!"

"Never!" Cook poured their tea. "It must have been the sounds of the other one in the bag that did it."

"Of course. They quite upset me, too."

"But he's a nice man. She'll get a good home." Cook sat down.

"Yes," Mrs. Blackburn agreed. "And it will be a treat for his children. Did you notice that the kitty's fur was just the color of Arabella's hair?" She put Miranda on the floor.

"It was the right thing to do," Cook said, staring into her cup. "His children need a pet."

Miranda took a brief look at the closed back door. She tensed her muscles and quick as a flash sprang through the pantry door, her bounding leaps echoing through the long hallway and up the stairs to Arabella's bedroom and the open window.

SIX

Arabella had never been so frightened in her entire life. From the moment she was carried out through the back door, terror overwhelmed her and even made her throat close up as if a tight hand were clutching it. She couldn't even whimper, so she concentrated on listening, hoping to hear Miranda's voice beside her and the tiny sound of Miranda running on the gravel path. But she heard only the policeman's heavy shoes clumping along the stones and the crackling rattle of the bag that was her prison.

The darkness inside the bag was blacker than Miranda's coat, without the glints of light that reflected on her hairs. There was nothing but a terrible, terrible blackness around her. She didn't know where she was being taken. She did know it was a vast region called the unknown. There, as all small animals know, many awful and horrible things might be waiting. She was afraid to move even the smallest muscle. She crouched in the bottom of the bag, listening to her heart pound in her ears. She could feel the hairs standing up on her back and could taste a thin wetness as specks of foam formed on her lips. The fear was almost suffocating as the close blackness of the bag pressed in on her.

Arabella tried to open her mouth to scream, but fear had paralyzed her completely. She sat, crouched and tense and very much afraid, as she was put into the bicycle basket and wheeled away from home on what would seem to her a long, long journey.

The swerving and rumbling of the bicycle were very frightening and made her so nervous she felt quite sick. She could no longer even hear her heart beating. But she knew she was still breathing (it was getting very hot inside the bag) even though she was too terrified to move.

Before Arabella was picked up again, her prison still as black as ever, the rumbling of the bicycle beneath her had ceased for a short time and then had begun again. Whatever the policeman must have stopped for, it certainly was not to let her out of the bag and head her in the right direction for home. And now her heart was heavier than ever. She knew there was no magic to help her out of this. Her fate was sealed in that brown grocery bag.

Now they were no longer cycling and she was being carried gently, no swinging back and forth or pumping up and down. Still she crouched in the bottom of the bag, her head bunched close to her shoulders, licking the foam from her lips and trying not to throw up. How much more would she have to endure? And where, oh, where was Miranda?!

"Children!" the policeman's voice called. "Anybody home?"

Arabella heard a door shut and a sudden babble of voices: "Papa!" "Papa's home!" "Mama, here's Papa!"

Something hard whammed into the bag, nearly knocking the breath out of Arabella.

"Hold on! Hold on! Don't jostle the bag! Where's Mama? Don't pull on me so, Ricky! You want me to fall down? Where's Mama?"

"Here I am. Did you bring us a wonderful surprise from the store? You're holding that bag the way you'd hold a baby. What's in it?"

There was a sudden hush. Arabella felt solidness beneath her and heard the crisp sound of the paper over her head. She opened her blue eyes as wide as she could get them and looked upward, waiting for the bag to open. This was the moment. She held her breath. And then a burst of light streamed through the top and fell onto her small shivering brown body.

Three faces appeared at the opening and peered down at her. It made Arabella quite dizzy to look up at the triangle of eyes and open mouths. She turned her head as far as she could, swiveling it like a lollipop, around and back around the other way. She stopped shaking and shifted her feet, inching her body in a circle, her neck arched as she stared straight up. "Oh, look," she said softly. "Children."

"Listen to it meow!" "It's beautiful!" "It's mine!" "Where did you get it?!" "Can we keep it?"

"Hold on! Hold on!" Policeman Barnes reached into the bag and brought out Arabella, cradling her in one arm and stroking her back.

"Is it mine?" The little girl who spoke was just the size Arabella had been before she changed over.

"Yours, Angel?" The policeman laughed. "It belongs to all of you together."

"And what made you think it would be yours?" asked the

boy called Ricky. Arabella looked down at him, noting he was smaller than the girl, and must be a little younger.

Angel lowered her head sheepishly. "I have the next birthday and I thought it might be my present."

Policeman Barnes held Arabella out to her. "You will get a present on your birthday, my little Angel. This is a gift from God for all of you. But you may hold her first, if you will be very gentle and promise to give Ricky and Dina their turns soon."

"I promise, Papa." Angel took Arabella and hugged her in her arms. "Is it a girl?"

"I think so. At least, at Simon Hall they called it a 'her.'"

The children's eyes got very big. "This is one of the cats of Simon Hall?" they asked in unison, their voices hushed in awe.

He nodded solemnly. "It was sent to you children as a present." He put his arm around his wife. "It's a nice present, isn't it, Mama?"

Mrs. Barnes smiled at him. "A very nice present. But I have no food for it. We have only enough milk for supper and their breakfast."

"Don't worry. I got a sack of grain sweepings at the feed store. All sorts of farm animals eat it and maybe cats do too. Anyway, it will keep her from starving. Tomorrow I will try to get a fish head at the river dock. And," he looked at Ricky, "there's another surprise for you. Something special from the cook at Simon Hall. Go look in the bicycle basket, Ricky." A sudden sadness crossed his face like a shadow.

"Ah," Mrs. Barnes said quietly. "Nothing new?"

He shook his head. "It's as if she had just vanished."

Mrs. Barnes put her finger to her lips. "Not in front of the children, my dear." She looked over at the sofa where the two little girls were cooing over Arabella. "The poor mother," she sighed. "I'll get supper ready now."

"I'll find a carton for the kitty," the policeman said. "She'll need a bed."

"What shall we name her?" asked the girl called Dina, who was about a year taller than the other two children.

"We'll think of something at supper. Come on now. Help Mama. We mustn't let her do all the work."

Of course Arabella had heard all this. She was very alert now that she was out of her prison and able to look about. She didn't know what it was that farm animals ate, but she knew what a fish head was and she certainly wasn't going to touch that! There had to be some way to escape. It couldn't, just couldn't be hopeless. The front door had opened, but quickly shut, as the boy, Ricky, went out. The windows were shut. There was no exit from this room . . . unless there was a hidden corner somewhere. She looked around. There were no hidden corners. In fact, there were no hidden anythings. It was such a small room that she could put the whole thing in just one end of her bedroom at home, the end with her playhouse and toys. Home. She wanted to go home. Her whiskers trembled. She wanted to be with her mother. And Miranda, Mrs. Blackburn, and Cook. And even Tom.

She began to cry pitifully, little whimpering sounds at first, but with each one she gained strength and they became louder and louder.

"You're squeezing her, Angel!" Dina tried to jerk Arabella from the little girl's arms, pulling her by her front legs, but Angel held tightly to the back legs, responding, "No I'm not!"

Arabella did not at all like being pulled from the front and the back at the same time and wailed loudly, her piercing cries reaching the ears of the girls' mother in the kitchen.

"What is it?" Mrs. Barnes asked, running into the room.

Ricky rushed in. "I could hear it from outside! They're hurting the poor cat!" He ran to the sofa, dropping the bags onto the floor and rescuing Arabella from his sisters.

Angel and Dina burst into tears. "We didn't mean to hurt her," they cried.

"There, there," said Mrs. Barnes. "The poor little thing's just frightened being in a strange place. You didn't do anything wrong." She picked up one of the bags, shook it, and put it aside. Then she opened the other. "What have we here?" She pulled out one of the cinnamon buns. "Oh, look. And I can smell butter in them, and just look at the chopped pecans all rolled inside."

"Butter and chopped pecans!" The girls stopped their sniffling and gaped at the bun as if it were a miracle.

"Why," Mrs. Barnes continued, "we haven't had anything so wonderful as this since . . . since last Christmas!"

"But it is like Christmas!" Angel exclaimed. "We got a present and now we have special treats!"

"So it is," their father said from the doorway where he had been watching them. "You girls come along and set the table. I don't want to have to say it again. Ricky can take his turn with the kitty."

"When shall we have the butter-and-pecan buns?" Ricky asked, stroking Arabella and wishing she would stop crying.

Arabella wished they would all pay more attention to her and less to Cook's cooking. After all, these were nothing more than ordinary everyday cinnamon buns. Cook made them all the time. Not that anyone ever got tired of them, or anything like that. Why, she even wished she had one right now, to take with her when she made her escape. Once she got out that door, she might find herself very hungry. It had been a long time since she had eaten. But first, she had to get out the door. She wailed again.

"Hush, kitty," Ricky said, giving her a little shake. "When shall we have them, Mama?"

"As soon as we eat our spaghetti and our greens. We shall have them for dessert."

"Yea!" The children shouted together.

Arabella stopped crying. Spaghetti! No wonder they were so happy. Even at Simon Hall she got spaghetti only on her birthday and on other very special occasions. She hoped it would have lots of yummy meat in the sauce, just the way Cook made it, and no mushrooms. She hated mushrooms. But what a strange thing it was to have buns for dessert! Surely there would be ice cream and cake if this were a special spaghetti night. She was very puzzled and cocked her head to the side, looking from one person to the other. Mrs. Barnes was still holding the bun; Angel was smiling and holding Dina's hand, and she was smiling, too; and Policeman Barnes was grinning very happily at all his family. She twisted her head to look up at Ricky, who was hugging her too tightly and hurting her ribs. All three children were just the right size to play with. If only I were still a girl, she thought, I could sit at the table and have special spaghetti with them and we could play games afterward. She bet they knew hopscotch and all those fun games she played at school. How nice it must be for them to have each other to play with. They must never get lonely . . . the way she used to get when her mother went away. Arabella cried again.

"Come on, girls," said Policeman Barnes. "Let's help Mama get supper out."

"I'll wait here with the kitty and try to keep her quiet," Ricky said.

"All right, but you'll have to go on the cleanup shift."

"Sure, Papa. I won't mind."

"And Ricky," Mrs. Barnes called through the doorway, "be sure and wash your hands before you come to the table. No telling what kind of fleas and dirt the cat has."

Fleas and dirt! No one had ever called Arabella dirty before! And fleas! There had never been a flea at Simon Hall! Humiliated and embarrassed, she let out a piercing wail. "I've got to get out and go home!" Such an unhappy Arabella. What would she do?

SEVEN

"She won't stay in the box, Papa," Angel said, leaving the table once more to put Arabella in the hard carton.

"She will when she gets sleepy," he answered. "Leave her alone for now. After supper we'll find a nice soft rag to put in the bottom. Don't let her onto your lap, Dina. Not at the table."

"What shall we call her?" Ricky asked.

"I like Kitty." Angel slipped back into her chair.

"Kitty? That's a silly name," Ricky said.

"It's not so silly," Dina said. "She's very beautiful. What's another word for 'beautiful,' Papa?"

"Pretty. But that would sound silly. My Italian friend at the police station calls beautiful things *bella*. What do you want to name her, Mama? Shall we call her Bella?"

"Kitty is nice. It's simple. And very easy to remember."
The children laughed and giggled.

"Do you think your Mama's funny?" The policeman

laughed with them. "All right, let's call her Kitty. Does everyone agree? We have to have a majority vote."

They all raised their hands.

"It's settled then. Well, Kitty, you have a name. Do you like it?"

"Oh, Papa, she can't answer you," Dina pushed Arabella down again.

Arabella wailed loudly, getting very cross that not one of them could understand her, even though they had come very close to getting her name right. And why didn't they put a plate of spaghetti down for her? No one had even asked her.

"Maybe she's hungry," Ricky suggested. "Can I get her a bowl of food?"

"What do you say, Mama? Shall we let Kitty eat in the dining room with us tonight?"

"I think she should get used to the kitchen. Put the bowl down next to the water bowl, Ricky. It will be her own feeding place."

"Any more spaghetti, Mama?" Dina asked. "I'm still hungry."

"Don't forget you have the cinnamon bun coming."

"I haven't forgotten." There was a pause before Dina spoke again. "I think you're right. I will be too full if I eat more now. Please, may I hold Kitty?"

"Push your chair back from the table," their mother answered.

Well, finally, Arabella thought. Now she could at least see what was going on. She sat up very straight on Dina's lap and looked at the table.

"There is more spaghetti, Papa," Mrs. Barnes said. "You should eat it up. You have to work the hardest of us all."

"After the children," he said.

"I believe they've finished. Angel is still working on the helping she started with. Ricky is getting Kitty's food organized. You're the only one left." She held out her hand for his plate.

"Thank you," he said.

Arabella watched the last pile of spaghetti being mounded on his plate. She blinked to make sure she saw correctly. Why, there was hardly any meat at all. Just a few little specks here and there, certainly no big gobs of it, the way Cook would have made it. She looked at Angel's plate. None there either. How queer. Didn't they like meat?

"Good, Mama," Policeman Barnes said, his mouth full.

"You make the best spaghetti there is. Three nights a week is not enough. I could eat it every night."

"I'm afraid there was little meat in the house . . . the end of the month, you know. It seems the prices go up every day at the store. Now butter is so expensive. And I know the children don't like dry bread."

"We don't need bread at every meal. This is good without it. Angel, you finish up those greens on your plate. Leafy vegetables have gotten to be like gold. We can't waste any of them."

Arabella watched Angel push a soggy green leaf and some spaghetti strands around on her plate until she had eaten them all. Angel looked at Arabella and smiled. "Hello, Kitty."

Arabella meowed, wondering why anyone had spaghetti three nights a week. That didn't leave enough times for chops or roasts or chicken croquettes or anything like that.

Policeman Barnes pushed his empty plate away. "Very good." He wiped his mouth on his napkin. "Someday, Mama, it will be Sergeant Barnes and then we can pay off the house mortgage and have steak once a month."

"Steak once a month!" Angel exclaimed in wonder.

"Don't give the children big ideas, Papa. We are very happy the way we are."

"Yes." "Yes." "Very happy." Angel and Dina shouted, joined by the voice of Ricky from the kitchen.

"I'm not deaf," their papa said, wiping his eye. "Come on out here, Ricky, and start clearing the table."

Dina stood up and carried Arabella into the tiny warm kitchen. "There you are, Kitty. A nice bowl of food."

Arabella stood stiff-legged in front of the bowl and stared

at the contents. She had never seen anything like it before—little hard nubby things that looked like a cross between a cooky and a rock, and bits of yellow corn mixed in with gray flaky things. Well, who knows, she thought, it might be good. She crouched low and, looking from left to right to make sure no one was going to snatch it from her, she gingerly took one dried brown piece in her teeth and crunched down. Oh, no! Yuck! Yuck! Yuck! She spit it right out onto the floor and began to cough. When she had caught her breath again, she wailed loudly and ran into the dining room and tried to jump onto the table.

"Down! *Down!*" Mrs. Barnes pushed her off. "You can't get on anything! I can't have your claws in things!"

"No, no, Kitty." Angel scooped Arabella into her arms. "You can't get on things and tear them." She pushed her face into the brown fur and whispered. "We don't have any money to buy new things. You have to be good, or we won't be allowed to keep you."

Arabella stopped wailing, and thought. No money? Is that why they didn't have meat? Or butter? Or cinnamon buns every day? She had always had so much—it had never occurred to her that there was someone who had no money. The children at her day school had the things she had. Well, maybe some of them didn't have quite as much. But everyone had money and meat and butter. She looked at the table. Did they have spaghetti so much because it was cheap? She had read many books about families with no money, and shabby children, and hungry pets. But she had never actually seen anyone who was poor.

The children drank milk, just the way she did. But where was a bowl of cream for her? Since she had become a cat, she had had a lot of cream. Cook would pour it into a dear little china bowl, and if she finished it in a hurry she would be given more. Was there no cream here? Was it more expensive than milk?

The thought of Cook, and home, started her crying again. She wailed and moaned loudly, instinctively reaching up to wipe away her tears, but finding only dry eyes. As everyone knows, cats don't shed tears. They just cry from a lonely heart.

"She's still frightened."

"She's hungry. Take her to the food again."

"Maybe she just screams all the time."

"Oh, no, not that," Mrs. Barnes exclaimed, throwing both hands in the air.

Arabella abruptly stopped. Screams all the time? Why, of course she didn't! That made her sound like a complete baby! Just what Tom had called her. How awful! Could she really be so terrible? She sat, very still and quiet and thoughtful.

"Angel has a calming effect on her," Policeman Barnes said. "Maybe we should give it to her for her birthday. No presents; just Kitty."

"Stop teasing her, Papa." Mrs. Barnes went to the corner and picked up her mending basket. "You put Kitty on the floor now, Angel, and help clean up the kitchen."

Angel put Arabella down. "What will I get for a present?"

"What would you like to have?"

Angel hung her head. "Would a new sweater be too much?"

"I'm just about to mend one Dina's outgrown. It will be like new for you."

"I have all Dina's old sweaters. I never get anything new."

Dina stuck her head around the kitchen door. "Be thankful you know who's been wearing them; mine all come from the secondhand store!"

"Girls!" Mrs. Barnes laughed. "Yes! I will get you each a new sweater. For your birthdays."

"Thank you, Mama." Angel kissed her mother's cheek.

"Now run along and help Dina and Ricky." She sat down in a chair in the living room and pulled a shirt out of the basket.

Arabella looked at the pile of old clothes in the basket. She was slightly uncomfortable with this family that was so poor. Oh, not that they weren't nice! And she could see they all loved each other very much and were very, very happy. She wasn't sure why she felt a little funny, but she did.

Without really thinking about what she was doing, she decided to jump into the basket. It looked so comfortable. That might take her mind off her misery for a little while. She took a big leap.

"Out! Out!" Mrs. Barnes grabbed her and unceremoniously dumped her onto the floor.

Arabella was startled. No one had ever bounced her around like that. She shook her head in quick little flicks, then started to wail again. She went from window to door and door to window, one little brown paw reaching out helplessly to touch the barriers, crying and wailing and meowing as loudly as she could. She wanted to go *home! Home!!*

"Mama," Policeman Barnes said. "I'm not going to be able to take this much longer. What should we do?"

"Maybe she just wants to go out. It's not so cold out anyway. Put her box and food and water just under the back steps. She will be protected there if it rains, and she can slip under the house if she gets frightened. With the food, she won't go far. We can let her back in in the morning. In time, she will settle down."

Arabella's heart leapt with excitement. She was being put out! At last, she could go back home!

Policeman Barnes cupped his hand around her plump little stomach and carried her to the kitchen door. "You're some kitty," he said a little gruffly, patting her head. "Out you go. And be here early. We may be able to spare a little milk for your breakfast."

EIGHT

Arabella flew down the Barneses' back steps as fast as her four furry legs would take her and scrambled to a stop behind the nearest big tree. Her heart was racing so fast she felt almost dizzy. She wanted to shout with joy, but she was afraid to make any noise for fear the policeman would rush out and capture her again, urged on by the cries of the children not to let her go.

There was another big tree a little farther on. She ran to it. And then to the next. And so on for five big trees. Then she relaxed a little and leaned against the rough trunk, oblivious to the bits of bark that caught at her brown coat and jabbed into her side.

"Oh, dear," she wailed softly. "Where shall I go? Everywhere I look is just the same. If only I can find the river, I can find home. But where do I start?" She tried to recall the bicycle ride for hints of which way they had come, but her mind was a blank. If only she had someone to ask. Miranda. Mrs. Blackburn. Anyone. She was just about to sit down and really cry loudly when she remembered Mrs. Blackburn's words: "Do you live far?" And Policeman Barnes's answer: "Just north of here."

She sighed with relief. That meant she wanted to go south. And she knew the river flowed south. Yes, she merely had to find the river. She took a step forward, then stopped. Which way was south?

Even though it wasn't cold at all, Arabella began to shiver in the night air, her eyes as round as the full moon that floated in the sky beyond the black treetops. If only Miranda were here, she would know what to do. The north star would give her a sign, but which one was it? She looked up through the trees, which patterned the sky like Mrs. Blackburn's dressy lace shawl. She couldn't see any stars because of the leaves! She must get into a field and try to figure it out.

Before she departed, she paused and peeped around the tree, looking back at the policeman's house, the lights from the windows glowing in friendly beams. Such a little house, but warm and cheerful, with happy people. They had been kind to her and had tried to love her. She got a lump in her throat thinking of them, probably just now eating their cinnamon buns as their special treat.

She turned and began her journey, half of her wanting to go back and look through the brightly lit windows. The other half wanted to get home—that would be *her* special treat.

She walked silently on the new spring grass dampened by night dew, threading her way beneath low-growing bushes and sliding in and out among fallen tree branches. She tried to stay in the moonlit patches, stepping carefully, not wanting to get scratched and poked. With every step, her apprehension grew. Once or twice she even thought of going back to the Barneses' house while she could still remember the way, but the thought of home made her push onward. She was sorry she had cried and screamed and wanted to be a cat. She wished she had listened to Tom and her mother and gone away to a school with other children. At least she would know where she was. As she thought of Dina and Angel and Ricky, she knew now that Tom hadn't meant to be mean to her. He really had thought it would be best for her to be with others her own age.

Her head was full of all these thoughts as she tried to find an open space so she could see the stars. Maybe she would come upon a road with a sign that said "South" or, best of all, the river, which definitely flowed south. She didn't hear the sinister creeping steps that followed her through the dark woods.

Suddenly a twig cracked behind her. As she stopped and looked back over her shoulder she heard a loud vicious snarling and saw eyes as red as flaming coals glaring at her. Her back arched high as her four feet came together and her hair bristled. She hissed in horror as the creature opened its huge jaws, the hidden lights of the night reflecting on long white fangs. With one mighty roar, it lunged forward. Arabella screamed and spurted ahead through the brush, twigs tearing at her coat, briars snatching tufts of hair from her body. Still it followed her, growling and snarling, its feet pounding the ground, sometimes so close behind her she could hear its panting and almost feel its hot breath steaming on her neck.

At first she screamed as she ran, but soon her breath came in short gasps and she sped silently under the brush and through the thickets, deeper into the woods. She headed into the denser growth, knowing instinctively that the huge creature would have a harder time getting through than she

did. Her heart was thumping so hard she thought it would burst, but onward she flew, using all her strength and endurance to outrun this monster behind her.

When she began to stumble and then falter, she knew she would have to give up soon. And then . . . What might happen to her was too terrible to think about. She pushed herself with one final burst of energy before she collapsed in a shuddering heap under the edge of a thicket of briars, where she waited in terror, her claws outstretched, her back hairs standing on end, her teeth bared like a very old and bad-tempered cat, ready to defend herself as best she could. She knew it would kill her in one loud snap of those mighty jaws, its fiery eyes burning into hers as it tore her to shreds. She became rigid with these awful thoughts, and waited.

She waited and waited.

But the monster didn't come.

After a very long time, she dared raise her head and listen. There was no sound. She must have outrun it.

At last, Arabella could stand up. She tested her legs, stretching them one at a time and giving them a little shake to make sure they were still working. She took a few steps.

She had no idea where she was. The lights that shone from the policeman's house were far behind her now. She would never be able to find her way back to their safety. No, there was nothing to do but keep going, even if it took her farther from home. The woods were very dark, the mass of treetops hiding the moon, and she was frightened. She stifled a sob and began to walk. And if you have ever been alone in a strange dark wood at night, you know just how she felt.

It wasn't long before Arabella heard a strange half-familiar droning sound, not steady like a swarm of bees or a running river, but a sound that came and went. She paused to listen, tipping her head from side to side, her ears perked forward. But the sound didn't come back. She walked on a little farther, and then she heard it again. She stopped and really concentrated. And then it came to her what it was. That had been the sound of cars! On a road! She jumped up and came down on all fours, her excitement making her meow with joy. If there really was a road, there might be a sign.

She hurried forward and soon stepped out of the woods right onto the dirt shoulder of a country road. "Oh, no," she cried, looking up and down the road. "No car will ever come along this old thing! But that's not true, is it?" she asked herself. "I'm quite sure I heard two."

Well, there certainly wasn't any sign of a car coming. Nor could she find a single road sign. And she would have been able to see that very clearly, as the moon was shining brightly down on her. She sighed. She was getting very tired. She had been running for a very long time. Now what would she do? She still had no idea where she was.

She looked down at herself. She was a mess. Her escape through the brush and briars had left her dirty and scruffy. There were still bits of bark in her coat and two burdock prickles stuck in her paw, one against the sensitive webbing between two toes. Luckily it didn't hurt. Mrs. Blackburn would have a fit when she saw her. Well, never mind that now. As soon as she got home, she would get cleaned up.

But that thought brought her back to the big problem: Where was the river and which way was home? There seemed to be nothing to do but continue walking and hope she was going in the right direction.

Being young and healthy, she was able to walk briskly despite her terrifying ordeal with that awful monster, whatever it was. Just wait until she told Miranda about it, she thought. And she would tell her the nice things too, like little Angel being just her age and Ricky and Dina being so sweet to her. And she would tell her about how poor the Barnes family was, and that there were even children who didn't get new sweaters every year. There was so much to tell Miranda. Maybe it would all go down in cat legend, and future cats of Simon Hall would talk about her adventures just the way they talked about poor loony Grandfather George in the north tower. And Mrs. Blackburn might learn of them too. Mrs. Blackburn knew lots of nice stories about the cats and about Grandfather George, though she had never told Arabella about *why* he was so loony. Only the cats knew that.

Arabella stopped and shook her paw. One burdock prickle was beginning to bother her. She bent and put her teeth around it and jerked, the bristly tips sticking in her tongue. "Yikes!" She sputtered and spit, shook her head, and spit again. "How nasty." She raised her head, looked around, and started off again, favoring the paw by stepping lightly on it.

After what seemed to be a very long walk, there still had been no road sign to indicate whether she was going north or south. She began to think she might never find one and would just keep walking and walking and walking, maybe all the while getting farther away from home. She sat down to think some more, sitting very straight with her paws close together, her little round haunches bowing out from her body.

Suddenly she heard a sound. Yes, it must be a car! She stood up and stepped right out onto the road, waiting, ready to hop in and be driven home. Surely it would be someone who would recognize her as one of the cats of Simon Hall.

The blinding lights approached, shining right into her eyes. She made herself as tall as she could, her head erect, tensed, anxiously waiting to be picked up, but then— horrors—the car rattled by so close that she had to jump back as the hot exhaust blew her fur up in bunches.

"Good heavens!" she exclaimed. "It nearly ran me down!" She watched the back of the car bump out of sight, a cloud of dust making her cough and sneeze. "What an awful smell! And why didn't it stop for me?"

"You're lucky you weren't killed," a voice snarled from the bushes behind her.

"Oh!" Arabella jumped and looked in the direction of the voice. Just at the edge of the woods she saw a very mean-looking cat with mottled gray fur cropped close to his body. "What a fright you gave me! Who are you?" But even as she asked, she felt a surge of happiness at seeing a fellow cat. If she had been a little girl she would have clapped her hands, but as it was she joyfully swished her tail back and forth.

"Never mind who I am. Why were you standing in the road? Do you want to be killed?"

"Of course not. I thought the car might give me a ride home."

"Home! Ha! You'll never see that again. And if you stand in roads, you'll never see anything again. Cars might stop for little girls, but no one stops for a cat."

Little girls? Arabella's eyes grew very large and she stared at the big gray cat. Not only was he mean-looking, he was just plain ugly. Was it possible he knew who she was? But before she could ask him, he walked out toward her.

"Follow me, you stupid ridiculous thing. I will show you something to help you remember to stay away from roads."

Arabella didn't think that was a very nice way to talk, but she followed the gray cat along the road, staying well away from the edge.

The gray stopped and pointed, glaring at her with his amber-yellow slitted eyes. "There."

Arabella stepped onto the roadway and peered ahead of her. She gasped. The furry russet tail of a small squirrel fluttered in the night breeze, the rest of it a flattened mat of hair mashed to the dirt like a thin rug. "Oh, poor thing. It's dead."

"Very dead. And perhaps you'd like to be the same way."

"What an awful thing to say! Of course I wouldn't!"

"Then keep away from the road." With that the gray turned away from her and started walking back to the woods.

"Where are you going?" Arabella ran after him. "Please don't leave me! Or at least tell me where I am!"

"Why should I tell you anything? I had to find out things for myself. You can do the same."

"But I need help. And you seem to know who I am. Or, at least I seem to think you do."

"What makes you think that? You're not so smart, you know."

"It was when you mentioned little girls. Do you know who I am? Oh, do please tell me."

"What if I do?" The gray stretched his front legs, his shoulders dipping toward the ground, and extended his sharp claws. When he righted himself, a low whistling hiss came through his broken front teeth. "You probably think I am an old cat, don't you? Well, I'm not. I'm not very old at all. But I have had to live in the world and survive by my wits. I have not been able to stay young, sleeping on soft beds and drinking sweet cream for breakfast. I have had to find my own way. So why should I tell you anything?"

The gray smirked. "When you have struggled awhile, you will learn that very little in life is nice."

"I don't believe that. I believe people and cats are nice and I think you should be nice too."

"Think what you want!" he shouted. Then he arched his back and hissed at her.

Arabella took a step back. "My goodness, why are you so angry all the time?"

"Go on about your business and leave me alone!" the gray cat snarled. "I should have left you to stand in the road and get killed!"

"Oh!" Arabella bit her lip and felt her heart thump. No one had ever hated her before. "I'll go right away if only you will tell me which way to go. I want to find the river so I can find my way home."

"It won't do you any good! There is no one there. The house is empty."

"Empty? But that can't be. No one would leave until . . . until . . ."

"Until what? Until the little girl comes back? Well, now they know that will never be. So everyone has gone." He sat down and began licking his paw.

"You *do* know who I am!"

"Of course." He looked at her with half-closed eyes. "You are a cat. Everyone knows the little girl is gone for good." He leered at her. "That is why they have gone away." He stood up and walked slowly toward Arabella, circling her, hissing into her ear. "There is no one waiting for you. They have all gone. People and cats. Cats and people. The great house is shut up. Closed. Empty."

"But that can't be! I was at home only yesterday. Or was it today? Oh, no! I can't remember when I was there! I'm all mixed up about time! Oh, no! Miranda told me yesterdays and tomorrows wouldn't matter anymore. But I never knew I would forget when something happened!"

"All gone," he hissed. "Your mother, your housekeeper, even your precious Miranda. All gone. There is no one left."

Arabella screamed and dashed to the woods. She sat down and began to cry very hard, wailing and sobbing with dry burning eyes and a heavy heart. Home. Home. She could see her room, the tall towers, the great steps that led to the heavy front door that opened onto the ancestral hall; she could smell the wonderful smells that came from the kitchen, and she could see dear Cook.

She cried so loud and so hard and for such a long time that she finally cried herself to sleep, the way creatures do to ease their distress, curled against a thick bunch of ferns that nestled close to the base of a tree and shielded her in their fronds.

When she woke up some time later, the first thing she noticed was the unbroken quiet. And then she remembered the ugly gray. Her heart swelled up again at his terrible words. She wondered if he had gone away. Nasty as he was, being with him was better than being alone. And he *did* know how to get her home.

She quickly sat up. Maybe he was mistaken. Maybe they hadn't left yet. If she hurried, she could catch them and stop them. There had to be a way to let them know she was safe.

"Are you still there? Hello?" She stood up and stretched her neck as far as it would go, looking all around her.

"Hello?" The prickle bothered her and she shook her paw. Then she walked back toward the road. "I'm sorry I don't know your name, but whatever it is, are you still there?" She looked up and down the long dirt road. "Oh, dear." She started to cry again. "Whatever shall I do?"

She began to trudge along. She knew she couldn't just stand there and wait for something terrifying to happen to her. Why hadn't she paid more attention to things when she was a little girl growing up? Tom was right. She was a baby.

She quickened her pace. Well, she would just have to grow up now. Somehow, she had to find her way. No more not paying attention. No more standing in the path of a car. She would follow the road for a while longer, then she would go back into the woods in search of the river. It would be dark there, and lonely. "But isn't it lucky cats can see so well in the dark," she said, trying to keep up her spirits.

"You're going in exactly the wrong direction," the now recognizable voice of the gray called to her.

"Where are you?!" Arabella cried out. "There! There! I see you now, on the other side of the road!" And without looking to right or left, she ran as fast as she could make herself go, across the road and to a hollow log where the mottled gray sat glaring at her with his evil amber eyes.

NINE

"Don't talk to me until I tell you you can talk!" the gray snapped at Arabella.

She sat down on the log, her tail curled to one side, the tip flipping up and down as she thought. She had never, absolutely never, met anyone so rude. He needed a good lecture, the kind Cook gave the delivery boy when he was hours late with the groceries. But Arabella didn't want to make the gray any nastier than he already was, so she kept quiet and thought. There must be a way to get him to talk to her and tell her how to get home. She wondered what Miranda would do under these circumstances. Time was of the greatest essence here: She had to get home quickly and stop everyone from leaving.

"Please, may I speak now?" she asked politely.

"It depends on what you have to say."

She thought quickly. Her blue eyes got very big and she turned to look at him very sweetly. "I wondered if you knew the Barnes children."

"No," he snarled.

"Have you ever met Cook, who lives at our house?"

"No!"

She jumped a little. "Cook likes to put tuna fish and chopped livers and kidneys," she almost gagged on this, "in little dishes for any cats that come around and want something to eat. I'm sure she would give you a whole big dish if you ever happened to appear at the door. The kitchen door, that is."

He turned his head and glared at her. "Livers and kidneys?"

"Yes. And cream, and milk with an egg beat up in it, and nice bits of hamburger and chicken, too." Her stomach began to grumble. "I'm sure if you ever happened by, you would find this quite true."

"No one has ever given me anything but trouble." He glowered at her, his forehead bunched above his eyes.

"I'm very sorry to hear that. But if you went to Simon Hall, you would find people who would give you something nice. Especially if you went right away."

"Ha!" He smiled his wicked smile. "If you think you can trick me into taking you home, you are mistaken. I am not easily taken in by silly promises and false hopes."

"If you had ever lived with a family, you would trust people more."

"It was living with a family that brought me this." He curled his lips back and bared his broken teeth. "See these two teeth? Knocked off right at the gum. And see my broken fang?"

Arabella instinctively reached out her paw as if to touch him, but he drew back. "What happened?" she asked.

"The family I lived with. The man got mad at everything and decided to take it out on me. He kicked me in the face. It broke my teeth."

Arabella gasped and hung her head and stared at the log. "I'm very sorry." She took a deep breath. "That was a terrible thing to do to you."

"That's not all," he answered, hissing at her. "People have done more than that. I have had a tin can tied to my tail, with the string so tight it almost cut off my tail, and everywhere I ran it clattered behind me until finally I ran it loose and it fell off."

"Oh, no. How awful."

"I have been kicked in the side and thrown into icy waters, by people who knew I couldn't swim."

"What did you do?" She didn't dare touch him. She trembled with shame for what humans had done to him.

"I finally bumped into a log in the river and climbed onto it and eventually it hit a bank and I got back on land."

"What terrible times you've had."

"I have had to go without food in the long winters and without shelter in the pouring spring rains. I have had to fight other cats in order to eat—that's how I got that piece of my ear torn off. And see this big scar on my shoulder?"

Arabella nodded, too saddened to speak.

"I tried to cross a moonlit field and a great horned owl almost made a supper out of me. But I was too quick for it, dodging to the side and ducking from its razor-sharp talons." He paused. "But why do I tell a stupid creature like you things of the world? You are ignorant and spoiled, not worth my time! Get away from me, you wretched child!"

"Why are you so awful to me? I haven't done anything to hurt you!"

"Go bother someone else!"

"Not until you tell me why you hate me!"

He flashed his snaggled teeth in the moonlight and hissed: "I hate you because of what you were, and what you gave up." His lip curled in contempt for her. "You had everything, everything anyone could want, and you were too spoiled to keep it. No, you had to give up your warm room and your daily fresh food and the people who took care of you and protected you, just to see what it would be like to be a cat. I despise you for what you had. Now get away from me." He turned his head and glared into the darkness. "Those black woods are my home, and when I am lucky I find a hollow log like this one to use as my bed. Now leave me alone. I told you you were headed in the wrong direction. That's all I'll tell you."

Arabella sat very still. Not even her tail twitched. She had listened to the gray's terrible pronouncements, and she knew they were true. No wonder he hated her. While he had starved and fought, she had sat around like a baby, crying because her mother was going to send her away to a school where she would be properly taken care of just the way she was at Simon Hall. How much she had to learn about the world!

Finally she spoke. "I am so very, very sorry to have heard all your awful stories. And I wish I could make your life easier for you. If I could only get back home and stop everyone from leaving, I could at least see to it that you have proper food."

"How do you think you will stop them? They will see only another cat. Only their little girl would have the power to stop them, and she is gone . . . GONE," he repeated with a loud growl.

Arabella's big blue eyes opened wide, her little mouth pulled in to a tight curve, and a wrinkly frown appeared high on her forehead. If only she could become a girl again, become herself again, her *real* self, she would be able to put everything right again. She could even help this mean sad old gray. "There must be something," she mumbled.

"Go away!" he shouted. He made a menacing move toward her, arching slowly and pulling up his shoulders. "Get out, or you will be sorry!" His claws shot out.

Arabella swallowed and spoke quickly, hoping her voice didn't sound as frightened as she felt "I won't go until you've told me the direction to the river." Then she held her breath.

"There! There! Through the dark woods!" He reached out a paw to strike her, but she jumped down and in a flash was running through the woods. And when you run for your life, you run very fast.

Finally she paused and looked back to make sure he wasn't following her. She listened carefully for any sounds, her ears twitching, laying back, then snapping forward with a quick twist. She heard only the beating of her heart and the hooting of a far-off owl. She recalled the big white scar on the gray's shoulder and listened again for the owl. It was very far away.

She sat down to think, licking her front paws, first one, then the other, pausing in between to listen and look, not bothering to remove the burdock prickle stuck in her paw nor the scraggly bit left between her toes.

When she felt truly safe, she relaxed and began to knead her claws in the soft springy moss beneath her—it helped her to think. She stayed on the alert, though, her ears making little movements to catch the slightest sound that might disturb her rest.

Her stomach grumbled, then made a squelching sound. She raised her head and looked down at her brown belly. She remembered she had been hungry quite some time ago, and now she was hungrier than ever. She would have to find something to eat soon. Very soon. She couldn't wait until she got home. Her heart gave a quick thump and she slowly and sadly got to her feet. It might be a long time before she made it back to Simon Hall.

She plodded heavily through the woods, listening to her stomach, feeling almost sick with hunger. Her eyes searched the ground around her, looking for something to nibble on until she could get a proper meal. How terrible it would be to be poor and not have enough to eat.

Just at that moment, a field mouse ran right in front of her. She put out her claws and grabbed it, dragging it toward her, her eyes flashing with greed. She meowed under her breath, the cat in her causing her to settle down on her stomach and pull the struggling mouse closer to her mouth. Just as she was about to sink her sharp little teeth into the sleek tan fur, the mouse squeaked pitifully. Arabella drew back and took a good look at it. Each of its ears was almost as big as its pointed face, its round eyes were shiny as jet beads, its long whiskers were twitching nervously.

Suddenly she screamed, "A mouse!" and dropped it, leaping to her feet. The startled mouse became confused and ran up her leg. Arabella screamed louder and shook her leg, jumping up and down, shrieking, "A mouse! A mouse!" all the while hopping about and trying to shake the mouse off her. Even when the poor mouse fell to the ground and

ran trembling to the nearest hole, Arabella continued to scream and shriek, and finally hurled herself onto a tree trunk and ran partway up.

And there she stopped, afraid to go farther up the tree for fear a great horned owl might be waiting in the branches for her, and afraid to go back down for fear the mouse would run up her leg again. She clung to the tree and screamed "Help! Help! Please, someone help me!" just the way any frightened little girl or kitty would do.

When she had worn herself out, she paused and dared to look down to see if the mouse had reappeared. But what she saw quite took away her breath! There, in a great ring all the way around the tree, were hundreds of pairs of yellow eyes. Pairs and pairs and pairs of slanted bright yellow eyes. And not just any kind of yellow eyes. They were the eyes of cats!

Arabella peered all around, first one way, then the other. Cats and more cats and *more* cats, all staring up at her. Suddenly from the outer circle of darkness one broke through the crowd, running toward the tree. This frightened her and she clawed her way farther up the trunk.

"Stop! Arabella, stop!" The approaching cat cried out in a voice so familiar to Arabella, it could have been her own.

"Miranda!" she called. "Is it really you?! Or is this a dream?"

Miranda stood at the base of the trunk. "It's no dream, child. Come down. Come down. No one here will hurt you. We have all been searching for you."

Arabella backed down as fast as she could and pressed her little body against the silky black fur. She rubbed up and down, sliding under Miranda's chin, curling her tail around Miranda's neck, then turning and sliding back the other way. Miranda purred and purred and when at last Arabella stopped, she began to lick Arabella, across her cheeks, her neck, her shoulders, and all the way back along her sides.

The other cats nodded their approval and sat looking on,

a gentle murmur going through their midst. All but one, that is. The snaggle-toothed gray edged his way to the front of the circle.

"No good can ever come from a human becoming a cat," he said sourly. "I told you so. She doesn't know our ways and never will. She has caused a great deal of trouble and will continue to do so. Look at her now," he snarled. "She doesn't care that we have spent half the night running over the countryside trying to find her." A ray from the moon lit up his face. The black slivers in the menacing amber of his eyes seemed to hang from the upper lids. "She should have stayed the way she was, but she was too ungrateful and self-centered to appreciate her life. She is too stupid to learn. She can only cause trouble for all of us this way. I say we ostracize her and never speak to her again."

A low threatening hiss arose from the throng of cats. "For shame." "Go away." "Leave us."

The gray curled his lip over his broken fang. "Mark my words. She will be nothing but trouble."

"No one asked you to come." The cats murmured. "You wanted to be in on the excitement." "If you had taken her home and gotten a reward, you wouldn't be saying that."

"She's trouble," he repeated, but he knew he was no longer welcome and slid away into the night.

"He's mean-tempered because he's been badly treated," Arabella said. "He told me all about it when he found me, way back by the road," though she had no idea how far away that was.

"Scum," Miranda muttered. "That cat has never had any character. He should have brought you to us the minute he found you. Let's go home now." With great dignity, she nodded her thanks to the ring of friends, who accepted her gratitude in silence and began to disappear among the trees in small groups and singly.

Arabella stood still, gazing after the gray cat.

"Come." Miranda pushed against Arabella and got her going in the right direction. "We must get home."

"He's had a very bad time. It might make any cat mean."

"Or a human," Miranda groaned a little as she started walking. "There are many evil humans and animals. They are usually that way because they have been badly treated. But that's the way of the world, and there's nothing we can do about it. Do keep moving. We are lucky to have a safe and happy home and I would like to get to it."

"But everyone . . . my mother, Tom, Mrs. Blackburn . . . are they still at the Hall or have they gone already?"

"Of course they're still there. People who love Simon Hall don't leave it if they can help it. Now be quiet and walk."

"What's 'character,' Miranda?" Arabella asked, wanting to hear Miranda's voice more than she wanted an answer.

"It's being able to count on someone to be always the same. That mangy mottled gray pretends to be your friend one day and the next would betray you for a fish tail, to say nothing of a head. Keep walking. I'm worn out with all this activity tonight." She spoke with a touch of exasperation, her head hung low, her shoulder blades sticking up from her back, her pace sluggish with limping steps. Then, looking at Arabella with compassion, her voice softened. "You must be quite tired out yourself."

"Quite!" Arabella fairly chirped, keyed up by the rescue and all her adventures. In spite of the bits of prickle still in her paw, she bounced on her pads as she walked, holding back to stay beside Miranda, her tail held straight up in the

air in a cheerful manner. "I was chased by a barking monster, but I outran it."

"Ah, a dog. It probably got bored and gave up."

"And I went entirely the wrong direction on a road and
almost got hit by a rattle-trap car and saw a poor dead squirrel," she rushed on with a torrent of words.

"You should have stayed back from the road." Miranda
turned her head and looked at Arabella. "Let's not talk now.
I am very tired. And we should walk silently and listen for
danger."

Arabella continued for a very few seconds in silence, then
she could stand it no longer. "How did all those cats know to
come looking for me?" she whispered.

Miranda stopped and stared at her. "They heard that the
little girl of Simon Hall was missing, so they were all on the
alert anyway. Then I spread the word that you, Arabella-cat,
were missing. Word spreads quickly among us, passing
swiftly from one to the next during the long night prowls.
Actually it wasn't so hard. One of them knew where the

policeman lived, and naturally we concentrated on that vicinity north of Simon Hall."

"But it was way on the other side of that road!"

"We were preparing to cross it when the night was deep enough to be sure there would be no cars. A wise precaution, you know. But then, we didn't have to, did we?" She smiled at the little brown cat. "You have been very brave, and I am proud of you. Now, let's go home."

"I'm going to eat something and go straight to my bed. My paw is still sore from having had a nasty prickle between my toes." Though it really was more annoying than sore. "Miranda, did you know that cream is too expensive for some people to buy?"

"Yes."

"How did you know that? We always have cream at home."

Miranda sighed. "I also know that many people are poor, like Policeman Barnes and his family, and don't eat as well as the cats of Simon Hall. And I'm glad you've found out. It's about time you learned a few things about the world."

"You're so wise." She tried to rub up against Miranda.

"I know. Keep walking. I need to get some sleep."

"Policeman Barnes's children never had a pet before. And now I've left them."

"We'll find a nice kitten and lead it to them."

"Oh! That would be ever so nice for them. When shall we do it?" she asked merrily.

"Not 'we.' I will put out the word. It will be done tomorrow."

"So soon? Where will a kitten be found so soon?"

"There are many homeless kittens. It will take less time to

find one than it will take to get you home. And that's not very far now."

"How far is it?" Arabella's voice rose with anticipation.

"Only a heart's wish away," Miranda answered quietly.

And Arabella wished with all her heart to be home, and soon the lights from the great mansion could be seen, beckoning them on.

TEN

"Oh, look!" Cook cried out as she opened the back door. "It's the little brown kitty come back! Mrs. Blackburn! Do hurry!"

"Well, finally," Arabella said. Deciding it was time to look pathetic, she limped past Miranda into the warm kitchen. "We're back where someone knows who we are." She looked at Miranda trudging through the door. "I hope she gives us something exceptionally delicious to eat. And, dear Miranda, isn't it grand that no one has left! You are here and so is Cook and, listen, I hear Mrs. Blackburn in the pantry now."

"Do stop that prattling, child." Miranda sank down to the floor for a brief rest. "I just want a little bite, then I'm off to bed."

"When I saw you in the woods, I knew you hadn't left me." Arabella looked all around with excitement in her eyes. "But I wasn't sure about the others."

"You should never have listened to that wretched gray. He just upset you for nothing."

"What's going on?" Mrs. Blackburn hurried into the kitchen.

"Just look who's come back!" Cook exclaimed, as she poured cream into two small china dishes. "It must be a sign!"

"Well, I don't know about that." Mrs. Blackburn bent down and lifted Arabella into her arms. "But I am glad she's back. We'll have to find another cat for the policeman. This one is meant to be here." She stroked the brown fur. "And where could she have been? Her coat is a mess. There are bits of bark in her neck and burdock prickles in her paw. She needs cleaning up."

"I say she needs some good food in her little belly. Give her to me." And Cook swept Arabella from Mrs. Blackburn's arms and put her in front of the dish of cream. "Now drink that, kitty. You'll soon feel better."

Mrs. Blackburn sat down at the table and watched the two cats drink their cream. "One of the old Mrs. Georges said never to turn away a cat who came in during a storm. And all this trouble," she choked a little and turned her head away from Cook, "is just the same as a storm. Yes, this kitty was meant to be here. It's something to do with her coloring, but I'm not sure what. Maybe time will tell."

"Well, I say she's come back to get a good meal." Cook busied herself cutting up a piece of chicken. "And that's just what she'll get." She put the chicken bits on a plate between Arabella and Miranda. "I hope someone is feeding our little one right now." And with that she shook her head and shuffled slowly to the sink.

Arabella stopped eating. "Isn't there *any* way we can tell them? It's too awful having them all so sad. Do you think my mother is still crying?"

"Probably."

"And Tom?"

"So it would seem. I can hear them in the dining room now, discussing you."

"You have awfully good ears, you know."

"I know." Miranda licked a splash of cream from her paw and ran her tongue around her little black mouth. "I'm going up to bed. Do try to be quiet when you come up."

"You're leaving me?"

"Yes. You're home now. Nothing can happen to you."

"Are you sure they won't put me out?"

"Quite sure." And she left the kitchen, through the pantry.

"Wait for me!" Arabella meowed loudly and ran after her. But when she came to the dining-room door, she stopped and looked into the big room.

The crystal chandeliers hanging from the vaulted ceiling were all lit up, and what seemed like hundreds of lights around the walls shone in their sparkling glass globes. Very large tapestries hung against the side walls in between the lamps, and big portraits of old George (the first) and his wife hung at either end of the long room.

Tom sat at one end of the table and Arabella's mother at the other. Little flames flickered from the candelabra placed along the table between the two of them.

Miranda had been quite right. Tom was talking about her. Arabella walked over to his chair and looked up at him and listened.

"But, my darling, I must talk about her. No, don't start to cry again. It is why I've said nothing before now; it pained me so to see you cry." He looked as if he might cry himself.

"I'm heartbroken the way it is; to mention her only makes it worse," her mother said.

"But I must. I feel a great shame. I feel responsible."

"Responsible? For what?"

"For her disappearance. Someone must have overheard our conversation about sending her away to school and told her, or perhaps she heard it herself. It was after that that she disappeared."

Her mother sat up very straight and put her hand over her mouth. "Can that be true?"

Arabella flicked her ears forward.

"I fear it is," he said. "She must have thought we didn't want her. And she ran away. If only I could get a message to her, if only I could tell her that we do want her, then maybe she would come back."

Oh, thought Arabella, if only I could! It's what I want more than anything! I want to be their little girl again!

"You mean—" Her mother leaned forward. "You don't think anything . . . well, you know . . . awful has happened to her?"

"No, *cara mia,* I think she is somewhere safe and doesn't want to come home. If only she knew how much I miss her."

Arabella rubbed against Tom's leg. "You're very close," she meowed at him. "Too bad you aren't a cat-person. Then you would know I've returned."

"Tom," her mother said, sitting up very straight, her voice brightening. "If she is safe, she might come home any minute. I'm afraid to get my hopes up, but it *might* be true."

"Of course it might be. It's just that I feel so rotten for having suggested sending her away."

"We will wait here until she returns." Arabella's mother lifted her chin. "And when she does, we might just decide to stay at home. It's been very comforting to be here. I'm sure our Arabella will come back to us if we wait. Don't blame yourself another minute."

"Thank you, my sweet." Tom absently stroked Arabella's head. "It has been a great worry on my mind."

"You have been such a help to me, Tom." Her mother brought her polished fingertips to her lips and blew him a kiss. "Since Arabella's father died, I really never thought I would be happy again. But despite my sorrow, I have been happy with you."

Arabella did think that Tom was being awfully decent to her mother. He could have just walked out when the commotion started, but he had stuck by her through it all. He probably did love her. Her mother must have been very lonely all these years. Maybe that was why she got married so many times and traveled so much, to keep from being lonely. Arabella realized she had never thought much about her mother or *her* happiness. But she certainly knew now that when you're lonely, you're very, very unhappy. She shivered just thinking of being alone in the dark woods.

She rubbed against Tom's leg again. She was glad he made her mother happy. If only he could get her to stop crying.

Tom reached down and touched Arabella's back. "Here is that little brown cat again," he said, gathering Arabella onto his lap. "She is not around as much as Miranda. I had forgotten about her."

"What brown cat?" her mother asked, peering past the candelabra. "I didn't know we had a brown cat."

"She came into the bedroom when you were lying down earlier. She's very beautiful."

"A little scruffy, it would appear from here. It has the same color hair as Arabella!" She choked and put her handkerchief to her eyes.

Tom's hands felt nice on Arabella's back, stroking her so gently. "*Que bella,*" he murmured.

Arabella knew that meant beautiful. The policeman had said it and she had heard Tom say it before.

"Bella," Tom repeated. "That's what we'll call her. Beautiful Bella. She is beautiful, even if she's a little scruffy. Shall we call her Bella, darling? Beautiful Bella?"

"That would be a lovely thing to call her, even if it is a

little redundant," her mother answered. "Bella. So similar to Arabella. I already feel she is one of the family." She sighed loudly. "She will be greatly loved if she stays here with us."

Arabella hopped down and walked to the other end of the table. She rubbed against the pale hand that hung limply by the chair. The slender fingers, smelling sweetly of lavender, stroked the little cat. "Run along now, Bella. Go on up to Arabella's room and find Miranda. She will take care of you. I want to sit awhile longer, Tom, darling. It's so peaceful here."

Arabella padded out of the room and into the great hall and started up the stairs. How good it would be to be back in her own bed!

"Miranda?"

The black cat twitched and shifted to her back, resting her head upside down on the quilt.

"Miranda!" Arabella shouted.

"Will you lower your voice! I am having a delicious dream about a little yellow warbler picking its way along a lilac branch. It is quite near my mouth now."

"Do wake up! I want to talk to you."

Miranda rolled over onto her stomach and opened her eyes. "I made it very plain I wanted to rest."

"But I need to talk to you. Please do wake up."

"What is it?"

"There must be some way we can tell my mother that I'm here."

Miranda was becoming exasperated. "All you think of is yourself. Will you please have a little consideration for the rest of us, namely me." The narrow yellow eyes regarded Arabella closely.

"I'm thinking of my mother. I'd like to tell her I'm all right."

"You can't."

"Can't?"

"How many times do we have to go over this? You cannot speak to a person who is not a cat-person."

"What will I do?"

"Don't start that wailing again. I'm going back to sleep and dream about that little warbler getting closer and closer."

"Oh, phooey on warblers. I'm talking about something more important."

Miranda stood up, arched her back, then faced Arabella squarely. "I noticed you ate some tuna shortly before you were taken away."

"Tuna? But tuna's a fish." She remembered it had been quite tasty.

"I know. And some time before that, I saw you sneak a piece of beef liver, thinking it was hamburger."

"No I didn't."

"Oh, yes you did. And you liked it."

Arabella meowed crankily, "You're horrid, Miranda, do you know that? Just horrid when you want to be. And why are you spying on me?"

"Not spying. Just observing. I must say, I think your tastes have matured."

"Observing what? That I have to eat those horrible things if I don't want to starve? That's what Cook gives us: fish and liver and raw chicken, ugh, and even a chopped-up gizzard, whatever that is, and I hate them all." She felt a twinge of shame as she said all this, thinking how fortunate she was that such bountiful dishes were always there without her asking for them. And, of course, so much cream!

Miranda yawned, her wide-open mouth showing the pale roof and rows of white teeth. "I know. And you don't know what you missed when you threw away that mouse. Don't worry about your mother and the others. Luckily they have you as a new cat at Simon Hall. If you had really disappeared, or gone away to school, they wouldn't even have that. Now stop talking. I am going to sleep." She lay down again and closed her eyes.

Arabella thought about this before she spoke. "Lose a daughter, gain a cat." She paused. "Being a cat's awfully nice—sometimes. That poor gray certainly doesn't think so, though. But being a cat at Simon Hall is different. Do you think a cat's as important as a little girl?"

Miranda opened one eye and fixed it on Arabella. "Do you feel important, as important as you did before?"

"I'm very sorry to have to say this, but I don't really."

"Why not? You do all the same things except go to school, and that was never tops on your list."

"That's true. All those numbers and spelling bees."

"So, what's really different? To you, I mean."

"I can't tell my mother I love her. In fact, I can't communicate with anyone except cats, and that's very limiting, you know." She sat down. "I guess I just want more than I can get by being a cat. Does that sound awfully selfish, Miranda? Miranda?" She put her head very close to the black fur. "Are you asleep again? Oh, dear, why do I always end up talking to myself?" She sighed and stretched out, resting her head on the soft pillow. "I'll hum to myself and put myself to sleep. Oh, I am so glad to be home! What did Tom call me? Beautiful Bella. For a moment there, when he called me Bella, I thought he was going to recognize me. I thought Policeman Barnes might, too. Bella, Bella, Bella," she hummed the word over and over. She was so very sleepy. Bella. Bella. Bella. She was getting even sleepier listening to herself humming and purring.

Purring? She opened her eyes. Purring? Was she really doing it? Yes, she was! She gave her tail a big swish and smiled. Then she closed her eyes and began purring again, thinking how very nice it was to be loved and to be home in her own big bed (which seemed absolutely huge), with her mother and Tom downstairs, and Cook cooking, and Mrs. Blackburn talking to her. Dear Mrs. Blackburn. . . .

"Arabella! Arabella!" The voice sounded so far away. "Arabella! Please wake up!" Now it was getting closer, like a voice coming through a thick fog. "Arabella! Answer me, child!"

Someone was shaking her shoulder. Arabella quickly opened her eyes and sat up. Mrs. Blackburn was standing over the bed, staring.

"Hello, Mrs. Blackburn," Arabella said, suddenly feeling strangely large.

"Arabella, where have you been?" the housekeeper cried, her face white with shock. "We've been searching for you everywhere!"

Arabella looked around her. The bed wasn't nearly as big as it had been when she went to sleep. "Oh, my goodness!" She looked down at the white skin on her hands. "And my legs!" she exclaimed. "They're so big!" She hopped down from the bed and almost stumbled as she landed on two feet. Quickly, she put her hands to her face, feeling a little giddy.

Mrs. Blackburn swept Arabella into her arms. "You've no idea how worried we've been!"

"But I do have an idea. I do, dear Mrs. Blackburn." Mrs. Blackburn had begun to cry, and Arabella felt tears well up in her own eyes. "And I'm very sorry to have worried everyone so much."

Arabella looked at Miranda, who was sitting up very straight and looking decidedly puzzled.

"I can't believe you're really here." Tears were running down Mrs. Blackburn's cheeks. "We've even had the police in!"

"Policeman Barnes," Arabella said softly.

"How did you know that?" Mrs. Blackburn released her, reeled backward, and collapsed onto the bedside chair, her legs sticking out straight in front of her with her shoes pointed up. Taking out her handkerchief, she blew her nose and stared at Arabella.

Arabella took a small step and swayed a moment before regaining her balance. She looked back at Miranda. "Miranda," she whispered. "What has happened?"

Miranda narrowed her eyes and sat very still, staring at Arabella.

"Miranda. Answer me, please. You know everything."

Still Miranda stared at her.

"Oh no!" Arabella cried. "You can't understand me! It's all been a dream! I haven't been a cat at all! Oh, dear Miranda!" She dropped onto the bed and put her arms around the black cat. "I don't know where I've been, but it's not where I thought it was!"

"Arabella!" Mrs. Blackburn sat up with a start. "You're delirious!"

"No! No I'm not! Oh, dear Mrs. Blackburn, I am so very happy to be at home and to be a little girl again."

Mrs. Blackburn quickly collected herself. "We must go and tell Madam at once that you've returned. Oh, my gracious. Just look at your hair! It has bits of bark in it and there are burdock prickles in your socks!" She put her hand over her heart and gasped. "Where *have* you been? I feel quite faint."

Arabella looked down at herself. "I really can't remember," she said, sliding off the bed. "Just look at me! I *am* a mess. Where do *you* think I've been?" she asked, her eyes getting very big.

"We'll talk about it later. The important thing is for us to tell Madam. She's been quite beside herself with worry." She stood up and reached out her hand to grasp Arabella's. "Come along. And you'd better come, too, Miranda."

"Yes, you certainly had," Arabella said to Miranda. "Oh, here I am talking to you again, just as if you could answer me. It will be *days* before I realize you can't."

Arabella was pulled into the hallway with a strong, swift motion as Mrs. Blackburn called loudly in a high shrill voice: "Madam! Madam! Madam! And you too, Mr. Fales!"

They went down the stairs to the second floor and along the hallway to the big staircase that led down to the ancestral hall.

"Madam! Mr. Fales!"

Arabella tugged her to a stop, and when the kindly but still-anxious eyes turned to look at her, she asked in a trembling voice, "Will they be very angry with me?"

Mrs. Blackburn put her arm around Arabella's shoulder. "What does it matter? You're home, aren't you?"

And down the steps they flew, with Miranda following a few paces behind, a quizzical expression on her face.

Arabella's mother and stepfather ran into the hall from the dining room, just as the door that led to the pantry flew open and Cook burst into the hall.

"Arabella!" they all shouted at once.

Arabella ran into her mother's open arms, and her own joyful cries were drowned out by the shouting and confusion in the hall.

The maid ran down the stairs, shrieking and whimpering, and the chauffeur and gardener both came rushing from some remote part of the house, all of them still up and about, hoping for news of their lost little girl. "Arabella!" "Arabella!" Her name was shouted until it rang from the vaulted ceiling.

"Oh!" her mother said when things had quieted down a bit. "I thought I would never see you again!" She hugged Arabella again and her pale skin took on a rosy glow.

Tom cleared his throat. "We should be very angry with you. You have given us quite a scare." Then he bent and kissed Arabella's cheek. "But we understand. And we have missed you terribly. Welcome home, my *bella*."

"Yes! Yes!" everyone cheered loudly. "Welcome home, Arabella!"

"And I have missed all of you!" Arabella cried jubilantly, wishing they would all stop shouting her name so much.

"We never meant to upset you," Tom continued. "Of course you mustn't go away to school. We want you right here with us."

"Yes, Arabella, darling," her mother said. "We'll be a real family at last. We'll never send you away to school."

"But you were right," Arabella said, prying herself out of her mother's arms and taking Tom's hand. "You should send me away to school. That was a very good idea of yours. I do need playmates." She looked wistfully at Miranda. "I'd like to be with other children. But only if you both will be here when I come home for vacations." She looked from her mother to Tom.

"Of course we will be!" they cried out. And her mother

added: "This is our home. This is where we want to be. This is where Tom and I will be happy."

Cook sniffed loudly and wiped her eyes on her apron. "I'm going right out and butter some of those rolls for you. And there are strawberries with cream. Oh, I do hope no one's eaten the apricot tarts!"

The gardener and the chauffeur and the maid all started talking again, thinking up things they would do for Arabella. Mrs. Blackburn was trying to answer Tom's questions. Arabella's mother was clasping and unclasping her hands and murmuring sweet things such as "lovely" and "so happy."

So Arabella scampered up the steps and sat next to Miranda. "I do love you so much and I really hate to say this, but I would rather be a girl than a cat. But, oh, you can't understand me, can you?"

Miranda gave Arabella her wisest look. "Of course I can. This is very interesting, I must say."

Arabella jumped back. "You *can* understand me!"

"So it would seem."

Arabella pondered the situation in silence for a moment. "You said once a cat, always a cat."

Miranda began to lick her front paw. "I know what I said."

"Did you make a mistake?"

Miranda raised her head archly and narrowed her eyes as tightly as she could without shutting them. "Mistake? Hardly. We have simply found a new dimension in cat-people. This will be a day to go down in the annals of Simon Hall. This is far more interesting than your adventures. *This* is the stuff legends are made of!"

Arabella put her arms around Miranda and hugged her; then they both began to purr.

"Listen to me!" she whispered loudly. "There's a fullness in my chest that seems to swell and vibrate, like a long laugh trying to escape!"

"That's rather what it's like."

"But I'm a little girl again!"

"I think you will have the best of both worlds."

"That's simply the nicest thing I *ever* heard. And just look at my mother and Tom and everyone we love, all down there talking at once. And look at the Grandfather Georges watching us. And see, Miranda," she said, pointing to the portraits, "I never noticed before that they were all smiling. Oh, I am so awfully glad to be home!"

*Arabella Slowly Turned Her Head
and Looked at Her Cat.*

"Can I become a cat? Is it actually possible?" she asked. It sounded positively *impossible*, but then, so did talking cats.

"Yes. Many things are possible." Miranda, the black cat, looked very wise.

"But how?" Arabella asked.

"Well," said Miranda in a very confidential tone, "you have to be a real cat-person to start with . . . ."

"Which you said I was."

"Yes. Then you have to want it with all your heart."

"I do want it. Please, Miranda." Arabella put her face close to Miranda's. "Please tell me what to do to become a cat."

"But, silly," Miranda said, rubbing her cheek against Arabella's, "you already are one . . . ."

Other Bantam Skylark books you will enjoy.
Ask your bookseller for the ones you have missed.

About the Author

LIZA FOSBURGH was born in Moultrie, Georgia, attended Mount Holyoke College, and now lives in upstate New York. A former editor, librarian, and housewife, she is the author of one adult novel, *With Friends Like These*, and numerous articles for magazines and newspapers.

The idea for *Bella Arabella* came from "having observed two large black cats for fifteen years. I came to suspect some hidden intelligence other than native feline."

About the Illustrator

CATHERINE STOCK is a children's book author, illustrator, and designer whose works include *Emma's Dragon Hunt; Sophie's Bucket;* and *Sampson, the Christmas Cat*.

She lives in New York City.